The Donkey on the Sands

and

Other Stories

by
ENID BLYTON

Illustrated by
Maureen Bradley

AWARD PUBLICATIONS LIMITED

For further information on Enid Blyton please contact www.blyton.com

ISBN 0-86163-849-2

Text copyright © The Enid Blyton Company
Illustrations copyright © 1996 Award Publications Limited

Enid Blyton's signature is a trademark of The Enid Blyton
Company

This edition entitled *The Donkey on the Sands and Other Stories*

First published 1996
Third impression 1998

Published by Award Publications Limited,
27 Longford Street, London NW1 3DZ

Printed in Hungary

CONTENTS

The Donkey
on the Sands

All the children knew the little, fat, grey donkey on the sands. He used to take them for rides at a penny a time, and would trot along at a fine pace.

"I kicked him on when I had my ride this morning!" said Jim to the others one day. "Goodness, you should have seen him gallop! He went about a mile a minute."

"You shouldn't have done that to him," said Nora. "He's a dear and always does his best."

"Pooh! You're just a silly girl," said Jim grandly. "You don't know how to treat horses and donkeys. My father wears spurs when he goes riding in uniform, and when he wants to make his horse go fast he uses his spurs."

"Well, I don't think it's right to hurt animals like that," said Nora, "especially things that really do their very best, like Neddy. He'll gallop without being kicked on."

But the boys thought it was grand to make Neddy gallop, so they all kicked and slapped him when they rode him. The donkey-boy didn't like it, but he didn't say a word.

It wasn't much good Nora saying anything either, for the boys only laughed at her and teased her. So she tried to make up for their unkindness by bringing Neddy a few titbits. She brought him a fine carrot, which he ate up in delight. She took him an apple, and he liked that even better.

He nuzzled his big nose into Nora's hand whenever the little girl came by. He flicked his ears and shook his tail with pleasure to see her. He was always glad when someone had given her a penny so that she could ride him.

The donkey-boy liked Nora too, and he gave her a much longer ride for a penny

than he gave the others. The others only went to the pier and back, but Nora went right beyond the pier to the breakwater. It was a very long ride.

Then the boys began to get cross because Nora had longer rides than they had.

"It's not fair!" they said. "If you go as far as the breakwater, we ought to too. It's not fair!"

"Well, you mistreat old Neddy and I take him carrots and apples, so it's no wonder he likes to give me a longer ride," said Nora. "Why don't you ask the donkey-boy if you can go as far as I do? He's the one who decides."

7

So that afternoon Jim went to have a ride, and he said to the donkey-boy, "I'll go to the breakwater beyond the pier."

"That will cost you twopence then," said the boy firmly. But Jim hadn't got twopence.

"You let Nora go as far as that for a penny," grumbled Jim. "It isn't fair."

"Well, she's good to the donkey," said the boy. "You're not. It serves you right."

Now Jim didn't like to quarrel with the donkey-boy for he was much bigger than Jim was – and he didn't dare to make the donkey go as far as the breakwater in case the boy made him pay another penny, which he hadn't got. So he just galloped off angrily, digging his heels into Neddy's ribs.

And because he couldn't do what he wanted to, he felt very angry with poor Nora. So he made faces at her, pinched her when no one was looking, and said horrid things about her to the others.

Nora had a bad time. John, Peter, Jim, and his sister Helen teased her all the time, and she was very unhappy. But the worst time came when they all went bathing one hot, sunny morning.

"Let's get hold of Nora and duck her under!" said Jim, with a giggle. "Come on – there she is out there. We can easily catch her."

"All right!" said John. "That will teach her to have longer rides on Neddy than we do!"

So the four of them waded out to where Nora was trying to swim. She did so badly want to learn, but it was rather difficult. Every time she took her feet off the sand to try and swim with them, she seemed to go under, and she hated that.

She suddenly saw the others wading out to her, and by the look on their faces she knew they were up to mischief. "What are you going to do?" she cried. "Go away!"

But they came nearer and nearer, wading up to their waists. Nora could not run away because there were horrid, muddy, sinking sands beyond her, and she didn't dare to wade out deeper because she couldn't swim.

Jim caught hold of Nora. He took a quick look round the beach to make sure that no mothers or fathers were watching. No – there was only Neddy and the donkey-boy, and they didn't matter.

Nora screamed. "Let me go! You horrid boy, let me go!"

"Come on, Helen! Come on, John! Let's all duck Nora!" called Jim, grinning. The little girl pushed him away as hard as she could, but she couldn't push all the others too. They came round her and caught hold of her swimsuit.

"Down she goes!" cried Jim. And down she went! How she spluttered and gasped and tried to catch hold of the others! The salt water went into her mouth and tasted horrid. She was frightened.

10

"Help! Help!" she called, getting up for a moment – but the others pushed her over again, and she sat on the sand with the water splashing her head.

There were no parents who could hear Nora – but there was Neddy! He pricked up his big ears, and knew at once that the others were teasing his friend. He shook himself free from the donkey-boy's hold and galloped down to the sea.

He trotted into the water and brayed loudly, "Hee-haw, hee-haw, hee-haw!" That was just to let Nora know that he was coming to help her.

11

Neddy went right up to the children, put his head into the water, and pulled Nora up. The little girl put her arms round him, sobbing. She climbed up on to his back, and Neddy trotted to the edge of the sea with her, and she got down safely.

"Oh, thank you, Neddy," she said – but Neddy hadn't finished his work. Oh no, there was plenty more to do yet! Back he trotted into the sea and went up to Jim, who couldn't get away from the big donkey in time. Neddy caught the boy by the back of his swimsuit and dragged him out of the water. Holding him firmly he stepped out of the water and took the wriggling Jim to a very muddy patch of sinking sand. He dropped him in – and there was poor Jim, rolling over and over in black muddy sand, trying his hardest to get out!

It was not very difficult to get out, really – but you should have seen Jim when at last he stood up and ran to firm sand. He was covered with black mud from head to foot! Neddy hee-hawed just as if he were laughing!

The Donkey on the Sands

Then he went to fetch John, and dropped him into the mud too. And he would have got Helen and Peter, but they ran home.

"Oh, Neddy! I didn't think you were so clever!" said Nora, squeezing the water out of her hair. "Those boys will never tease me again – and I guess they won't tease you either!"

They didn't. Neddy had taught them such a lesson that not one of the children dared to tease Nora or to hurt Neddy again. Wouldn't I have loved to see him galloping into the sea to rescue Nora!

The Very Strange
Secret

There was once a goblin who made himself a great nuisance to everyone. He borrowed this and he borrowed that, but he never returned anything. He said spiteful things, he pushed and pinched and knocked the small fairies about, and he never did a kind deed for anyone.

"If only we could send him away," groaned the folk of the village where he lived. "He is a perfect nuisance."

"Let's go to him and tell him he must move," said Dame Flinders.

"He would only laugh at us," said the others.

"I think I've got an idea!" said Nidnod, a sharp-eyed, sharp-eared pixie. "Listen!"

Everyone listened.

"We'll pretend that we've got a very

strange secret," said Nidnod. "We'll have a meeting about it. It shall be a secret spell to get as much gold as we want – but really the spell will be one that will make anyone fly out of the window to the moon!"

"But what do you mean?" cried Dame Flinders. "How will that help us?"

"Don't you see?" said Nidnod. "We will not ask Green-Eyes the goblin to our meeting – but we will leave the window open so that he can hear everything. And we will say among ourselves that this spell will make anyone rich, and so Green-Eyes will go home and try it. But it won't make him rich – it will only make him fly out of the window!"

"Ho ho! What fun!" cried the pixies. "We will meet here tomorrow – and, Dame Flinders, be sure to let Green-Eyes know about it so that he can come and listen. Then we will see what happens! Nidnod, look up the flyaway-to-the-moon spell, so that you can say it to us tomorrow."

Off went everyone, and old Dame

Flinders, who lived next door to Green-Eyes, hobbled off too. Green-Eyes saw her coming back, and he called over the wall, "Where have you been?"

"Never you mind!" said Dame Flinders, knowing that that would make Green-Eyes very curious indeed.

"What have you been talking about?" said the goblin.

"Aha! We've something to talk about tomorrow, I can tell you!" said Dame Flinders. "It's a very strange secret!"

"Tell me," said the goblin, jumping over the wall. "Is it a new spell?"

17

"Haven't I said you're not to come into my garden," scolded Dame Flinders, ignoring his question. "It's marvellous the way my lettuces and carrots walk out the moment you walk in! Get back to your own side of the wall, Green-Eyes."

"Not till you tell me what you're going to talk about with the others tomorrow," said the goblin. "And why haven't I been asked to come, I'd like to know?"

"Perhaps because you're not wanted," said Dame Flinders.

"Oho, so that's it, is it?" said Green-Eyes. "Well, I shall come to the meeting, so there!"

"You don't know where it is," said Dame Flinders. "And you won't be allowed in if you do come; so there!"

"Ah, we shall see!" said the goblin. He picked six lettuces and went back to his house, making up his mind to follow Dame Flinders the next day and see where the meeting was to be held. Then he would listen and hear what the very strange secret was! It must be a new spell. Oh yes, he would get that secret and use the spell before anyone else! That would punish them!

The next day Dame Flinders put on her hat and coat and went down her garden path at twelve o'clock. Green-Eyes was watching, and he slipped after her. She went through the wood until she came to the pixie Hoho's little house. Green-Eyes saw many other folk going in too. So that was where the meeting

was to be held. Good! He would wait until everyone was safely inside, then he would creep up to the window and listen!

Soon the door was shut. But one of the windows had been left open. Green-Eyes crept underneath and pricked up his big, pointed ears to listen. The folk inside saw the tip of one big ear and grinned to each other. So the goblin was safely there, listening. Ho ho, he should hear what the very strange secret was in a minute!

"Folks!" said Nidnod, standing in the middle of the listening people. "You are here today to learn a very strange secret.

It will tell you how to get as much gold as you want. Then you will be rich, and able to do exactly as you please. We have not asked Green-Eyes the goblin here because we don't want him to share in our luck."

The goblin's big ears twitched angrily, and the people inside saw the twitching and wanted to laugh. But nobody did – they were so afraid of spoiling everything.

"This is the very strange secret," said Nidnod, and he pulled out a paper. "This is what you must do. Find a red-spotted toadstool, a peacock's feather, a butterfly's wing that is wet with dew, a scraping off a witch's broomstick, and a soap-bubble blown in the sunshine. Mix them all together, and then put them on the fire. Something will come down the chimney – aha!"

"Yes – gold will pour down the chimney!" chuckled the goblin, rubbing his hands. "Gold! Ah, I've got their very strange secret, and I'll use it straightaway for myself. And what is more, I know where all the red-spotted toadstools are! I'll pick them every one, so that not one of the pixies will be able to find one for the spell! Then I shall be the only one in this village to be rich! And I'll take everyone for my servants and make them work hard from dawn of day to midnight!"

He ran off, chuckling. He picked every single red-spotted toadstool and took them home. He took a peacock's feather from his jar of feathers, found a butterfly's wing and dipped it in dew, ran to Witch Heyho's house and cut a scraping from her broomstick, and last of all blew a soap-bubble in the sunshine. He mixed everything together, and to his great surprise the soap-bubble did not burst but took all the other things into itself and bounced about the room with them inside!

"Very strange," said the goblin. "I don't quite like it. This doesn't seem like a gold spell to me. It reminds me of some other spell. Oh, well, I can't be bothered to look it up – it must be right if Nidnod told the others. Here goes the bubble into the fire! Now I'll look out for the gold to come pouring down the chimney!"

All the pixies who had been to the meeting had collected near the goblin's house to watch what would happen. They were delighted when they saw him picking all the toadstools and blowing the bubble in the sunshine.

"He is making the spell!" chuckled Nidnod. "He thinks it is going to bring him gold! Ho ho!"

Green-Eyes watched the bubble go into the fire and then looked up the chimney to see the gold he hoped would come pouring down.

But none came! Instead there came a most tremendous wind that blew the goblin right over on to his back. Then the bubble flew out of the fireplace and began to grow enormous! It bounced over to where the goblin lay, and in a trice he was inside it. Then another great gale of wind blew down the chimney and the bubble flew to the window.

"Oh! Help! Help! I've made a flyaway spell!" shouted the frightened goblin. "Help! I thought I was making a gold spell! I'm blowing away!"

"You shouldn't have listened to our very strange secret!" shouted the pixies, dancing out into the road. "It's your own fault! You've made yourself a flyaway-to the-moon spell! Goodbye, Green-Eyes, goodbye! Give our love to the Man in the Moon, won't you, and tell him we don't want to see you any more!"

The big bubble whirled away into the sky, taking the goblin with it. The great

wind blew after it, tossing it higher and higher. At last it could no longer be seen.

"Well," said Nidnod, "he's off to the moon! It will be a long time before he's back again! It serves him right. He shouldn't have such long ears!"

Green-Eyes hasn't come back again yet. He's having quite a long stay with the Man in the Moon!

A Little Bit
of Magic

Fanny had been reading a book of fairy-tales. My goodness, the magic there was in Fairyland! The way wizards changed people into different things – and the way that spells were worked and magic done – it was wonderful!

"Oh, Mummy!" she said, when she had finished the book. "I wish I could see some magic. But I don't believe there is any nowadays. Things don't change suddenly into something else – there don't seem to be any spells about at all."

"Well, I can show you something that seems like magic," said her mother. "Something that happens a hundred times every year, in everyone's garden."

"Show me, Mummy!" said Fanny, really excited.

So her mother took her out into the garden. She went to the cabbage patch and hunted about. She turned back a leaf with holes in and showed Fanny a green-and-yellow caterpillar there.

"We'll take this caterpillar on a piece of leaf, and watch him use a spell to change himself into something else," she said.

So she and Fanny took the little caterpillar to Fanny's bedroom on a piece of cabbage-leaf. Mother found a box and made holes in it. She put a piece of glass over the top so that Fanny could watch the tiny creature eating his cabbage-leaf.

"Has anyone told you what a caterpillar can turn himself into?" asked Fanny's mother. But Fanny was only six, and she didn't know.

"Well, this caterpillar can turn himself into a butterfly with wings," said Mother.

"However can he do that?" said Fanny in surprise, looking at the long caterpillar. "I can't see the beginnings of any wings at all."

"He hasn't got even the beginnings now," said her mother. "He gets those later when the magic begins to work. We will watch him each day."

So they watched the caterpillar. Twice he grew so fat that he had to change his tight skin. Fanny was surprised to find he had a new one underneath each time. She gave the little caterpillar a new cabbage-leaf every day and he grew and grew.

One day he didn't want to eat any more. He went to a corner of the box and began to spin a kind of silky web there. Fanny couldn't think where he got it from.

But he had plenty of silk. He fixed himself safely in the corner – and then a strange change came over him. He changed his skin for the last time. He lay still. He became hard and brown. He seemed quite, quite dead.

"He seems just a hard little case," said Fanny, puzzled. "He isn't like a caterpillar any more. But he isn't like a butterfly either. His magic must have gone wrong, Mummy."

"We'll wait and see," said Mother. "We call him a chrysalis now. Watch carefully each day."

30

Fanny watched – and one day she was very excited. "Mummy, Mummy! I believe there is a butterfly being made inside the caterpillar's hard brown case! I can faintly see the outline of wings – and what looks like new legs all bunched up together! Look!"

Her mother looked – and as she looked, a magical thing happened. The case split down the back! It began to move and wriggle – and, suddenly, out of the split came a small head!

"Something's coming out – something's coming out! Look!" squealed Fanny.

Something did come out – something with four white crumpled wings, six thin legs, and a head with pretty, trembly feelers on it! Something so unlike a caterpillar that it was quite impossible to think there had ever been a caterpillar inside the case.

"It's a pretty white butterfly!" said Fanny. "A butterfly with wings! Mummy, how did it grow wings? It hadn't any when it turned into a chrysalis. How can a caterpillar turn into a butterfly? Do, do tell me."

"I don't know," said her mother. "Nobody knows. It's a little bit of magic. The caterpillar goes to sleep and wakes up as a butterfly. It's like the tale of *Beauty and the Beast* – you remember how the ugly Beast turned into the beautiful

Prince? Well, that's the same sort of thing that the caterpillar does."

"It's real magic," said Fanny, watching the butterfly dry its crumpled wings in the sunshine. "Soon it will fly away and be happy in the flowers. It won't eat cabbage-leaves any more. It's a butterfly!"

Have you watched this bit of magic? You ought to. It's just as strange as anything that happens in Fairyland, isn't it?

The Very-Full Stocking

Once upon a time there was a fat kitten called Fluffy. He lived in a little house with his mother and father, and had a lovely time. They spoilt him dreadfully, because he was their only kitten, so he had all the cream that was on the top of the milk, plenty of sardines, and half of his mother's kipper at suppertime.

Now one Christmas night he was very excited. His mother had promised that he should hang up his stocking and that in the morning he would find it filled with all kinds of good things.

"But you must go to sleep quickly, or you will find your stocking empty in the morning," said his mother.

He went to sleep quickly. He didn't hear the tiny mouse that lived in the hole in the wall come creeping out. He didn't hear the mouse sniffing to see if there were any crumbs on the floor.

The tiny mouse was hungry. The cats didn't leave very much for him to nibble, and he was always terribly afraid of being caught. He came out each night, and sometimes he was lucky enough to find a crumb or two, and sometimes he wasn't.

Tonight he smelled a most delicious smell. It was the smell of cheese, sardines, kipper, and lots of other things. Wherever could they be?

The little mouse ran to the end of Fluffy's bed. Good gracious! The smell came from there! The mouse stood up on his back legs and sniffed harder.

"What a strange thing!" thought the mouse. "Fluffy's stocking is crammed full of delicious things tonight! Never before has there been anything in his stockings – but tonight one of them is quite full. If only I could creep up and have a nibble!"

Well, it didn't take him long to clamber up the bedclothes on to the bed. He ran to where the stocking was hanging on the foot of the bed, and stood up to sniff.

But alas for the poor little mouse! He stood on one of Fluffy's paws! And, of course, that woke up Fluffy at once. Fluffy sat up, wondering who was treading on him – and in a trice he flicked out his paw and caught the trembling mouse!

"Let me go, let me go!" squeaked the mouse in fright.

"What were you doing on my bed?" asked the kitten.

"Only smelling at all the good things in your stocking," said the mouse. "That's all. It's a wonderful stocking you have tonight."

"Is it?" cried Fluffy in surprise, and he too began to sniff. "Dear me, yes – my

stocking is full of the most delicious things to eat. How dare you come and sniff at my Christmas stocking, mouse?"

"I'm very sorry," said the mouse. "But it's such a marvellous stocking I couldn't help it. Please do let me go."

"I'll let you go if you can do something impossible," said Fluffy with a chuckle, for, like all cats, he loved to tease mice.

"What's that?" asked the mouse in fear.

"Well, you see my stocking, don't you?" said the kitten. "Now, it's quite crammed full – there's not a corner to push in anything else. If you can put something else in my stocking, you may go free! If you can't, I'll eat you for breakfast."

The little mouse thought hard, his

heart beating fast. Then a fine idea came into his tiny head.

"I can put in something else," he said.

"You can't," said the kitten scornfully. "Why, not even I could – so I'm sure you couldn't."

"I can," said the mouse.

"All right. Go on – try," said the kitten, and he took his paw off the little mouse. The mouse ran to the stocking. He stood up on his hind legs and nibbled away at the bottom of the stocking, at the toe. He nibbled and he nibbled.

"What are you doing?" said the kitten

angrily. "That's not putting anything else in my stocking."

"Wait," said the mouse. "Wait." And he nibbled again at the toe.

"Mouse, stop nibbling," cried the kitten. "You are spoiling my stocking. Unless you tell me *at once* what you are going to put into it, I'll catch you again!"

"Kitten, use your brains," said the mouse cheekily. "I have put something into your stocking that wasn't there before – I have put a hole there! There's always room for a hole, no matter how full a stocking is!"

And without waiting to see what Fluffy would say, the mouse leaped off the cot, ran to his hole and disappeared. Fluffy was angry.

"Putting a hole into my stocking!" he said. "What next! Bad little mouse! I'll eat him next time I see him!"

But he didn't get the chance, for as soon as Fluffy was fast asleep once more, the mouse came creeping from his hole with two big bags. He went to the end of the bed and, standing on the floor, he waited for the things in the stocking to fall through the hole he had made at the end.

A bit of kipper fell through. That went into the mouse's bag. A whole sardine fell out, and then a piece of Cheddar cheese. Those went into the bags too, and soon they were quite full.

The mouse gave a squeak of delight and ran back to his hole. He put on his new hat, tied a scarf round his neck, for it was a frosty night, and set out to find a new and safer hole, carrying with him enough food to stock a nice big mouse-larder for a week!

I don't know where he went to – but I can't help hoping that such a clever little creature found a good home, and lived happily ever after!

The
Enchanted Goat

Once upon a time a great fair came to the village of Penny-Come-Quick. There were roundabouts, swings, coconut shies, conjurors, clowns, and a score of other splendid things. Little Benny Biggles was so excited that he couldn't sleep for thinking of it all.

He went every single day, and of all the wonderful things at the fair there was one that he simply couldn't take his eyes off. This was a wooden goat with wings on each of its heels.

A Chinaman was in charge of it, and if any one paid fivepence he would make the goat rise into the air, fly round the fairground and then come back again to him. Benny could have watched that all day. He thought it was the most wonderful thing he had ever seen.

"I wonder how it does it?" he said to himself. "Wouldn't I love to ride on it!"

Now no sooner did he think that than his heart began to beat very fast indeed. Why shouldn't he have a ride on the goat?

"I'll just see if I can!" said Benny. So the next day, when the Chinaman was taking fivepences, Benny stood as close to him as he could to see what he did to make the goat fly off.

"It's easy!" said Benny to himself. "Why, he just pulls one ear back, that's all! I could do that myself!"

When the Chinaman's back was turned, and he was telling everyone about his wonderful goat, Benny crept up to it.

"My goat, he will fly all round the fair," said the man. "Give me just one more fivepence and you shall see him go!"

Benny suddenly leaped on the goat's back. All the people cried out "Oh!" in surprise, and the Chinaman turned round quickly. When he saw Benny on his goat, he ran towards him, shouting out something in a strange language that

the boy could not understand.

But before he could get to the goat, Benny pulled back its right ear. In a second the wooden creature rose into the air, all its foot-wings flapping hard. Benny hung on tightly, his breath taken away.

"Ooh!" he cried. "What an adventure! Go on, goat, go on!"

The goat flew right round the fair-ground, and Benny could see everyone below staring up at him in the greatest astonishment. The people pointed their fingers at him, and shouted to one another.

"See! A little boy is riding the enchanted goat!" they cried.

Benny expected the goat to fly down to the Chinaman after it had gone round the fairground once, for that was what it always did. He thought that the man would be cross with him, but he didn't mind that! He had had the loveliest ride in all his life!

But oh dear me! The goat didn't go down to the Chinaman! After it had circled round the ground once, it suddenly rose much higher in the air and started flying straight towards the setting sun! Benny was too surprised to say anything at first, and then he gave a shout.

"Hi! Stop! You're going the wrong way, goat! Take me back to the fairground! Hurry up and turn round!"

But the goat took no notice of Benny at all. It went on flying towards the sun, very fast and very straight. Benny began to feel frightened. He clung on tightly to the goat's horns, his hair streaming out behind him. Below him he could see fields and hills stretched out very small, like a toy countryside. He saw a train going along a railway line, and it seemed to him to be smaller even than his own clockwork train at home.

"Stop! Stop!" he shouted to the goat. "You are taking me too far! Turn round and go back to the fair!"

Still the goat took no notice. Benny kicked its wooden sides with his feet, but that didn't do any good either. Whatever was he to do?

On and on went the goat, faster than ever. Soon they came to the sea. When they were right over it, the little boy looked downwards. He saw dark blue water stretching out all around him. Soon

45

no land was in sight at all. Benny had no idea that the sea was so big. He clutched the goat more tightly, afraid that he would fall into the water far below.

The sun sank down into the western sky and darkness came. The stars twinkled brightly, the moon came up, and Benny grew very sleepy. He began to cry, for he was afraid.

"I wish I knew how to stop this goat," he sobbed. "I expect it will go on like this for ever and ever, and I'll go round and round the world till I fall off."

Then he dried his tears and began to think hard.

"If I pull the right ear back to start the goat, perhaps I push it forward to stop it," he thought. But before he did anything, he peeped downwards to see if they were over land or sea. They were still flying over the water, but Benny could see an island not far off. He decided to try and alight on that.

He pushed the goat's right ear forward. Nothing happened at all. The goat still went steadily on. Then the little boy took hold of the left ear, and pulled that back. At once the goat began to slow down!

"I've found the secret, I've found the secret!" cried Benny in delight. "Oh, if only I'd thought of that before!"

He peered below him, and saw that the goat had not quite reached the island, but would land in the water round it. So he quickly pushed the left ear forward again, and pulled the right ear back. The goat at once flew straight onwards. When he was exactly over the island, Benny pushed the right ear forward and pulled the left ear back.

The goat flew down to the land. Benny tried to see what it was like but he could see little, except that he thought he could make out a huge building of some sort. Nearer and nearer to the land came the goat, and at last it was skimming along just above the ground. Then *bump*! It landed, and stood quite still while Benny got off.

The little boy saw that he was at the edge of a wood, but it was so dark that he knew it was no use trying to find anyone to help him. He must wait till the morning. He stretched his stiff legs and yawned for it was long past his bedtime and he was very sleepy.

Then he felt for the goat's ears. He carefully pushed the left ear forward and made certain that the right ear was in its proper position too. Then he found a soft patch of heather and, curling himself up in it, he went fast asleep.

It was day when he awoke, and the sun was shining in the eastern sky. Benny looked around him in surprise, for at first he did not remember how he had arrived there. Then he saw the wooden goat standing near by, and he remembered everything.

"Ooh, I am hungry!" he said, jumping to his feet. "I wonder where I can get something to eat. Then I'll jump on to my old goat and go off home. If I fly to the east, I'm sure to get there sometime. As soon as I see the fairground beneath me,

I shall fly down to it!" He looked round him. He could hear the sound of the sea nearby, and he remembered that he was on an island. Behind him was a wood, and to the right was a very high hill – almost a mountain. On the very top was an enormous castle with thousands of glittering windows.

"Good gracious!" said Benny in astonishment. "Whoever lives there?"

He saw a smaller hill nearby, and after carefully hiding the wooden goat under a bush, he started off to go to the top. When he stood on the summit he looked round him. He saw sea on every side, for the island was quite small. It had two hills, the one he was on, and the very high one on which the castle stood. A little wood lay between, and from the very middle of it rose some smoke.

"Someone must live there," said Benny. "I'll go and ask them if they would kindly give me something to eat, for I've never been so hungry in all my life before!"

Down the hill he went, and into the wood. He soon found a little path and

followed it. After a while he came to the strangest house he had ever seen. It was quite small, and was built of precious stones which glittered so brightly that Benny was almost dazzled. Round it was a circle of white stones.

Benny walked up to the circle. He stood outside, trying to see the door of the cottage – but he could see none, though he walked all round it several times.

"Well, I'll just have to go right up and see where it is," said the little boy. So he put his foot over the ring of white stones to walk up to the house.

But good gracious me! He couldn't put it on the ground again! It was held there in the air, though Benny could not see anyone or anything holding it. Then all at once there came the noise of a hundred trumpets blowing and a thousand bells ringing!

"Oh my! Oh my!" said poor Benny. "This must be a magic circle or something!"

Suddenly there came a voice from the house. Benny looked, and saw a gnome's head peeping out of a window.

"Who are you?" demanded the gnome. "You have put your foot in my magic circle, and started all my bells ringing

and trumpets blowing. Take your foot out."

Benny tried to but he couldn't.

"I can't," he said. "Please undo the spell or whatever it is. I'm getting so tired of standing on one leg. I'm only a little boy coming to ask for something to eat."

"Say your sixteen times table then," said the gnome, sternly.

"Oh, I can't," said Benny, nearly crying. "Why, I'm only up to seven times at school; and I don't know that very well yet."

"Oh, that's all right then," said the gnome, smiling. "I thought you were a wizard or a witch disguised as a little boy. If you had been, you would have known your sixteen times table, but as you don't, I know you are a little boy. I've taken the spell off now. You can come into the magic circle."

Benny's foot was suddenly free. He stepped over the ring of white stones and went up to the glittering house. He looked everywhere for a door, but he couldn't find one.

"Clap your hands twice, and call out 'Open, open' seven times!" said the gnome.

Benny did so, and at once a door appeared in the wall and opened itself in front of him. The gnome looked out and pulled Benny inside by the hand. At once the door disappeared again.

"Why do all these things happen like this?" said Benny, puzzled. "Am I in Fairyland?"

"Not exactly," said the gnome, setting a big bowl of bread and milk in front of Benny. "This island was once part of Fairyland – just the two hills and the wood, you know – and a great giant came and built his castle on the top of the biggest hill."

"I thought giants weren't allowed in Fairyland," said Benny in astonishment.

"They're not," said the gnome, putting a hot cup of cocoa by Benny's side, "but this one was very cunning. He turned himself into a small goblin, and built a tiny castle. Nobody minded, of course, for there are lots of goblins in Fairyland.

But one night he changed himself back to his proper shape, a giant as tall as a house, and made his castle grow big too! What do you think of that?"

"Go on!" said Benny, eating his bread and milk. "This is very exciting!"

"Well, the giant was so big and so powerful that the King and Queen couldn't get rid of him," said the gnome. "He was a terrible nuisance, because he would keep capturing fairies and taking them to his castle. Then he would charge the King a thousand pieces of gold to get them back again."

"The horrid monster!" said Benny.

"Then, as they couldn't make the giant go away," said the gnome, "they suddenly thought of putting a spell on the land he owned, and sending it away to the middle of the sea to become an island! So they did that, and off went the two hills and the wood one fine starlit night! They landed in the sea miles away with a terrible splash, and here we are!"

"But how did you come to be here?" asked Benny, puzzled.

"Well, I happened to have built my house in the wood without anyone knowing," said the gnome, sighing. "So, of course, I went too, and I can't get back. The giant was in a terrible temper when he found what had happened. He came tearing down to me, and if I hadn't quickly put a spell round my house, he would certainly have turned me into a hedgehog or something like that."

"And does he live here all alone?" asked Benny.

"No, he has got seven fairies with him," said the gnome. "The King didn't know that he had stolen them on the very night his castle was moved, so of course the poor things are still there. I wish I could rescue them; but there is such a powerful spell all round the castle that I couldn't get near it even if I tried all day!"

"What does he do with the fairies?" asked Benny, finishing his bread and milk to the very last crumb.

"They are his servants," said the

gnome, "and very hard he makes them work, I can tell you. If they are not quick enough for him, he beats them, and I have often heard them crying, poor things. But they will never be rescued, for no one can get to the castle."

"What a shame!" said Benny. "Oh, how I wish I could rescue them!"

"You're only a little boy," said the gnome scornfully, "you couldn't possibly do anything."

Benny looked at the gnome. Then an idea flashed into his head.

"Tell me, Mister Gnome," he said, "is there a spell on the castle top as well as all around the walls?"

"Of course not!" said the gnome, staring at Benny in surprise. "The castle is much too high for anyone to get on the top. Why do you ask?"

"Because I think I can rescue the fairies!" said Benny, his heart beating very fast. "I've got an enchanted goat here, which I came on, and I believe I could make it fly to the castle roof and, if I could only find the fairies quickly, they could mount on its back and I could take them away with me."

"An enchanted goat!" said the gnome in astonishment. "Then you're not a little boy after all. I'll put a spell on you if you're a witch or a wizard!"

"No, no, don't!" cried Benny. "I really am a little boy. Listen and I'll tell you how I came here."

In a few minutes the gnome knew Benny's story. The little boy took him to where he had hidden the goat, and the gnome grew tremendously excited.

"Oh, Benny!" he cried. "I believe we'll do it! Oh, how grand!"

"Will you come with me?" asked Benny. "I feel a bit frightened all alone."

"Of course I will!" said the gnome. Then he and Benny got on to the goat's

back, Benny pulled the right ear back, and off they went. They flew high above the castle, and then Benny made the goat go downwards.

The castle had a flat roof, and it was quite easy to land there.

"Talk in whispers now," said the gnome. "If the giant hears us, we shall be captured at once. Look! there are some steps going down from the roof. You'd better go down them and see if you can find any of the fairies. I'll wait here."

Benny ran to the steps. He climbed down them very carefully. They went round and round and down and down. At last he came to the end and found himself in a long passage with doors opening off.

"Oh dear! Had I better try each one to see if the fairies are inside?" thought Benny. "No, I won't, I'll go on to those stairs over there, and go down a bit further. If the fairies do the work for the giant, they may be in the kitchen."

He went down some more stairs, and then down some more. They seemed to be

never-ending. At last he heard a
tremendous noise. It came from a room
nearby. The door was open, and Benny
peeped in. He saw an enormous giant
there, lying in the biggest armchair he
had ever seen. He was fast asleep, and
the great noise Benny had heard was the
giant snoring.

"Oh, good!" thought Benny in delight.
"Now I can look about in safety for the
fairies."

He came to a smaller door, and listened.
He thought he could hear the murmur of

61

little voices behind, and he opened the door. Yes, he was right! Sitting round a big fire, polishing enormous mugs and dishes, was a group of small fairies. One of them was crying.

When the door opened, they all sprang to their feet expecting to see the giant. When they saw Benny, they were so astonished that none of them could speak a word.

"Shh! Shh!" said Benny. "I've come to rescue you! I've got an enchanted goat up on the roof. Hurry up and come along with me. I'll take you back to Fairyland."

The fairies were so full of joy that they ran to Benny and hugged him. Then they ran lightly out of the room and up the stairs, treading very softly indeed when they passed the room where the giant slept. Benny followed them, and at last they all reached the roof. The gnome stood there with the goat, and greeted them in delight.

How they hugged one another and smiled for joy! Two of the fairies wept for gladness and Benny had to lend them

his handkerchief to dry their eyes.

"Come on," said the gnome, at last. "We mustn't stop here. If the giant wakes he will be sure to miss you and put a spell on you somehow. Are you all here?"

Benny counted the fairies.

"Good gracious!" he said in dismay. "There are only six of them! Didn't you say there were seven, Mister Gnome?"

"Oh, where's Tiptoe, where's Tiptoe?" cried all the other fairies. "We've left her behind! She was watering the plants in the greenhouse, and we've left her behind!"

"Well, call her," said the gnome. "If the giant wakes it can't be helped. I expect she will get up here before he knows there is anything the matter."

So all together the fairies called her:

"Tiptoe! Tiptoe! Come up to the roof at once! Tiptoe!"

A little voice from far below answered them. "I'm coming!"

Then suddenly there came a thunderous roar. The giant had woken up!

"WHO'S THAT CALLING!" he shouted. "YOU'VE WAKENED ME FROM MY SLEEP, YOU WICKED FAIRIES! I'LL PUNISH YOU, I WILL!"

"Ooh!" said the fairies, turning pale.

"It's all right," said the gnome. "By the time he's looked into the kitchen and called for you a few times, we shall be gone! Look, here's Tiptoe!"

The seventh fairy came running up the steps to the roof. In a trice the others explained everything to her.

"Get on the goat," said the gnome, "the giant is getting very angry indeed."

The fairies began to clamber on the goat – but whatever do you think! There was only room for five of them! The goat was much too small.

"Oh my, oh my!" groaned the gnome. "I

don't think I've time to make it big enough for us all, but I'll try. Stand away everyone."

He drew a chalk ring round the goat, clapped his hands, and began to dance round and round it, singing a magic song. Little by little the wooden creature grew bigger.

The giant below was roaring more angrily than ever and then Benny suddenly heard his footsteps coming up the stairs! "Quick, he's coming!" he shouted. The gnome hastily rubbed out the chalk circle with his foot and ran to the goat. He pushed Benny on first and then he helped all the fairies on. Last of all he got on himself, though there was really hardly room for him. Just as they were all on, the giant appeared at the opening to the roof.

Benny pulled back the right ear of the goat and at once the animal rose into the air. The giant gave a tremendous roar of anger and surprise, and fell down the steps in astonishment. By the time he

had picked himself up, and was ready to work a powerful spell on the goat to bring it back, it was far away in the sky.

Benny was trembling with excitement, and so were all the others. For a long while no one spoke. Then the fairies all began to talk at once, and thanked Benny and the gnome over and over again for rescuing them. Benny listened to their little high voices, and thought them the sweetest sound he had ever heard.

After a long time he looked below him. To his great astonishment he saw that he was flying just over his own home! Away to the right was the fairground, and the music of the roundabouts came faintly to Benny's ears.

"Oh, I think I'll go down here," said Benny. "There's my home, and I would like to see my mother and tell her I'm all right. Do you mind if I get off here? The gnome will take you safely back to Fairyland."

So down they all went, and Benny jumped off the goat at the end of his own garden.

"Goodbye," he said. "And would you mind sending the goat back to the Chinaman at the fair! I expect he will be upset not to have it."

"Certainly," said the gnome, "we can easily do that. Well, thank you for all your help, Benny. Goodbye!"

"Goodbye, goodbye!" called the fairies, as the goat once more rose into the air. Benny watched them until he could no longer see them, and then ran indoors to tell his mother all his adventures.

"I must go to the fair tomorrow to see if the fairies have sent the goat back," said Benny. And the next day off he went. Sure enough, the goat was there – but will you believe it, the gnome had forgotten to make it small again, and it was simply enormous!

The Chinaman was so astonished! He couldn't make it out at all.

"It is a very strange thing!" he said, over and over again. "Who can tell me what has happened?"

Benny told him – but he needn't have bothered, for the Chinaman didn't believe a word of his story! He took his enchanted goat away after the fair was over, and, as far as I know, nobody has ever heard of him since.

Bonzo
Gets into Trouble

Bonzo was a rough-haired fox-terrier. He was a clever little fellow, and very fond of his little master, Peter, and of his big master, Peter's father.

He would do anything in the world for them. He played ball when they wanted a game. He lay quietly by the fire when they wanted to read. He walked for miles with them when they wanted a walk. He welcomed them with delight whenever they came home from school or from business, and jumped up and barked at the top of his voice to show them how glad he was to see them.

One Saturday afternoon Peter's father said they would bath Bonzo in the sunny garden.

"He is dreadfully dirty," he said to

Peter. "He really must have a bath. Get the old tin bath out of the shed, Peter, and I'll get some pails of hot water."

"I'd better catch Bonzo first," said Peter. "He hates baths, and he'll run away and hide if he sees the bath coming!"

But Bonzo had already heard the dreadful word "bath"! He ran into the kitchen and hid under the table. Peter found him there and tied him up to the table-leg to stop him hiding anywhere else.

71

"You stay there and be a good dog," he said. "We'll make you so nice and clean that Mummy won't even mind you sitting in the best armchair!"

Peter went to get the tin bath. Then he found the shampoo, the scrubbing brush and the old towel. His father was carrying pails of hot water to and fro.

Bonzo watched angrily. Why couldn't he be dirty? It was nice to be dirty. A bath was a horrible thing to have. He wouldn't have one – no, he wouldn't! He'd bite through his lead and get away!

He began to gnaw his leather lead. He bit and nibbled, gnawed and tugged – and at last, hurrah, it was in half! He gave a yelp and tore out of the door. He

72

knew a fine hiding-place in the garden bushes. He would go there and wait until Peter and his father were tired of calling him.

Off he went, and managed to get to the bushes without anyone seeing him. He sat down and kept as quiet as a mouse.

Soon the bath was ready. "Get Bonzo!" called Father. Peter went to get him – but dear me, he was gone! There was the lead bitten in half, and no Bonzo!

"Oh, Daddy, isn't he naughty? He's gone!" cried Peter. "He's bitten his nice new lead in half, and now I shall have to open my money-box to buy a new one. Where do you suppose he is?"

"Goodness knows!" Father said crossly. "I'll whistle him and perhaps he'll come." So he whistled. But no Bonzo came. He heard the whistle quite clearly, but he thought of the bath waiting for him and he made up his doggy mind that he wasn't going to move!

Peter whistled. His father whistled again. Then he called, "Bonzo! Bonzo! Come here, Bonzo!"

Then Peter called, "Bonzo, Bonzo, Bonzo! Good dog! Where are you? Bonzo, come here!"

No Bonzo came. Father called again, getting really very cross, "Bonzo! Bonzo! Bonzo! *Bonzo*!"

Bonzo trembled to hear such a big voice, but he didn't move. He crouched down in the bushes and waited.

Peter's father was very angry. He began to look for Bonzo. He hunted everywhere and so did Peter. The bath water got colder and colder. Soon it was too cold to be of any use.

At last Peter and his father gave up looking for the naughty little dog. They emptied the water out of the bath and went indoors. Bonzo crept out of the bushes and went to the open window. He lay down underneath to listen to what they were saying in the room beyond. Were they very angry with him?

"That wretched little dog is a perfect nuisance," said Father. "It's too late for you to go and fetch me my magazine now, Peter. I must go without it."

"Oh, Daddy, let me go," said Peter. "It won't take me long."

"No, you can't go now, Peter," said his mother, looking up from her knitting. "I'll be getting our tea ready in ten minutes."

"I do think it's horrid of Bonzo to behave like this," said Peter. "I've got to buy him a new lead, and he's made Daddy and me waste all the nice sunny afternoon, and now poor Daddy can't have me fetch his magazine for him as I always do. I think Bonzo is a horrid, naughty little dog."

Poor Bonzo! He felt as if his heart was breaking when he heard his little master speaking like that! He hadn't thought of Peter having to buy him a new lead – and he had quite forgotten about Peter always fetching his father's weekly magazine. Dear, dear, no wonder they thought him a horrid little dog. Well, he would go in and beg for forgiveness. Even if they told him off he wouldn't mind. He was so sorry about it.

So in at the door he crawled, his tail between his legs. Peter saw him and cried out in surprise, "Look, Daddy, look, Mummy, here's Bonzo! I wonder where he was hiding. He looks awfully sorry for being so naughty."

"Take no notice of him," said Father. "I shan't tell him off. It will be a much bigger punishment for him if we take no notice. Don't pat him or speak to him."

So nobody spoke to Bonzo at all. Nobody patted him, nobody even looked at him. It was perfectly dreadful. Bonzo had such a pain round his heart that he really thought it must be breaking into small pieces. Whatever could he do to make his master and mistress love him again? Oh, how he wished he had never run away from his bath!

He licked the big master's fingers, but Father took his hand away. He crawled over to Peter, but Peter wouldn't even look at him. He went to Mother, but she took no notice at all.

What could he do to make things right? How could he show everyone that he was sorry? He lay in a corner with his shaggy head on his paws and thought and thought.

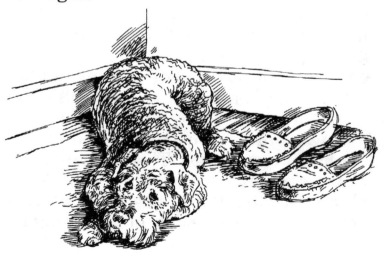

77

And then he had a fine idea! He would go to the shop himself and get the magazine! He knew the way, and he could bring the magazine back in his mouth if he was careful not to bark.

Bonzo jumped up and went into the hall. He knew that Father always put a round yellowish thing called a pound on the hall table, which Peter took to the shop with him and gave the man in exchange for the magazine. He had better take that little round thing with him in case the man in the shop wanted it.

He jumped up on to a chair and tried to reach the pound coin with his mouth. He knocked it on to the floor and jumped down to pick it up. At last he managed to get it into his mouth. Off he went, out of the open kitchen door, the pound safely in his mouth.

It was quite a long way to the shop, but he got there at last. There was nobody in the shop except the owner, who was reading a book. Bonzo pushed open the door with his nose and went in. The man looked up.

"Hello, Bonzo," he said. "Is Peter coming for his father's magazine? I've got it here, ready for him."

Bonzo jumped up and dropped the wet coin from his mouth on to the counter. The man was surprised. "So you've carried the money for Peter, have you?" he said. "Well, I never!"

The man waited for Peter to come, and when the little boy didn't arrive he went to the door and looked for him. He wasn't anywhere to be seen.

"That's funny," said the man, puzzled. "Where is Peter?"

Bonzo sat up and begged for the

magazine. He thought the man was very stupid not to understand that he had come for the magazine. The man picked up the pound coin from the counter and scratched his head, puzzled. What ought he to do?

"Wuff!" barked Bonzo impatiently. "Wuff, wuff!" The man suddenly took up the magazine he had put ready for Peter, folded it and held it out to Bonzo. In a trice the little dog snatched it from him, held it firmly in his mouth and trotted out of the shop. The man gaped in astonishment and ran to the door to watch him scamper down the street.

Bonzo raced home. He didn't talk to a single dog on the way because he was so afraid that if he opened his mouth to bark he would drop the paper. He still had it safely in his mouth when he reached home. He ran in at the kitchen door and went into the living-room. He went up to Peter's father, his tail wagging hard, and dropped the magazine into his lap.

Father picked it up in astonishment and looked at it. "Look!" he said. "Bonzo's

brought me my magazine! Do you think he's been to the shop for it?"

"Wuff, wuff, wuff!" said Bonzo, frisking round, longing to be patted.

"I'll see if the money is gone from the hall," said Peter's mother. She went, and came back saying, yes, it had gone! Then the telephone rang, and it was the man ringing up from his shop to tell Peter's father about how Bonzo had come to his shop with a pound and had taken the magazine!

"I'll call Peter," said Father. "We must tell him about Bonzo going to the newsagent's on his own."

81

So Peter came downstairs, and dear me, how surprised he was to hear what Bonzo had done.

"I know why he did it, Daddy," he said. "He heard us talking about the magazine, and he made up his mind to go and fetch it to show us he was sorry for being so naughty about his bath. Didn't you, Bonzo?"

"Wuff, wuff, wuff!" barked Bonzo, and licked Peter's hand in joy.

"Well, well, we must forgive him," said Father, stroking the happy little dog. "He

was certainly very clever to think of doing that! And fancy his taking the money, too! I think he had better go and fetch my magazine every week, Peter, as he knows so well how to do it! It will save you going."

Bonzo was very happy. Peter's father patted him, his mother stroked him, and Peter tickled his neck. Everybody loved him again, and he wasn't in disgrace any more.

And now every Saturday he goes to fetch Father's magazine for him. He takes the pound coin in his mouth and brings back the magazine neatly folded. The man in the shop thinks he is a very clever dog, and each week at the shop if you were there you would find three or four people waiting for Bonzo to come, so that they might see him do his little bit of shopping!

Tomorrow Bonzo is going to have a bath. I do hope he won't run away again, and get himself in disgrace!

Goblin Magic

Now, once Hurry wanted some water from the well, because he was doing his washing and he needed to rinse it. So he called to Scurry, his friend.

"Hey, Scurry! Fetch me some water from the well, will you?"

"No, I won't," said Scurry. "Especially as you don't even say 'please'. Go and fetch it yourself."

"Well, I will," said Hurry, in a temper, "and what is more, I'll make you carry it, so there! Dinkle-um-ducket, change to a bucket. Dinkle-um-dell, off to the well!"

And hey presto, poor Scurry found himself changing shape. His legs disappeared, so did his arms. He grew a thin, curved handle. He was a bucket!

He couldn't say a word, of course. He

was just a pail to carry water in. Hurry grinned and picked up the pail by the handle.

"So you said you wouldn't go to the well and carry back water for me, did you?" he said. "Well, you're going after all, and you'll come back carrying plenty of water for me to use. Ho, ho, ho!"

But halfway to the well Hurry met someone he didn't like at all. It was the goblin Crookity. Crookity called to Hurry:

"Hey! Always in a hurry, aren't you? Wait a bit, I want to talk to you."

But Hurry wouldn't wait. He ran ahead as fast as he could, swinging the pail. Crookity ran after him.

"Hey! That's a funny pail you've got! Something strange about it, isn't there?" he cried.

"Yes, there is," said Hurry, fiercely. "I've changed Scurry into this pail, see? So you be careful I don't change you into something."

"You can't," said Crookity. "Nobody can. You know that. I'm too clever at magic for anyone to play a silly trick like that on me."

Hurry knew that was true. Everyone was scared of Crookity because he knew so much magic. Nobody liked him, but nobody could get rid of him. Hurry scowled at him.

"You think you're so clever, do you? Well, you couldn't have changed Scurry into a bucket. I don't believe you could even change yourself into one!"

Clang! Crookity leaped high into the air, and came down with a loud clang. He was a bucket, just like Scurry – without even a magic word either.

Then the strange little bucket giggled, and leaped into the air. When it came

down, it wasn't a bucket, it was Crookity again.

"Clever. Very clever," said Hurry. "I couldn't work magic as quickly as that. Can you change yourself into a – a broom, say?"

Swish! Crookity jumped high in the air, and came down again with a swish – but now he was a big broom, and dear me, he swept Hurry right off his feet so that he fell down with a bump. The broom laughed loudly, leaped into the air and there was Crookity again!

87

"That was very funny," said Crookity, enjoying himself. "What shall I turn into next?"

"Oh dear. I don't know. Well – what about a – a – let me see – I can't think – well, what about a teapot?" said Hurry, getting scared.

Thud! Crookity leaped up into the air, and came down with a thud. He was now a very large teapot, and out of the spout came a cloud of steam. And then, oh dear, the teapot tilted itself and poured hot tea all over poor Hurry! He yelled and ran away, and the teapot bounced after him.

But it laughed so much that it couldn't pour.

It leaped into the air, and when it came down again there was Crookity, rolling over and over on the ground, roaring with laughter at his joke. Hurry scowled at him. He picked up his pail. He had had enough of Crookity.

"No, no, you mustn't go," said Crookity. "Tell me something else. You say you want water in that bucket, which is really poor Scurry. Shall I change into water and fill the bucket – and then throw myself at you, and drench you? Ho, ho, ho!"

Splash! He leaped into the air once more and came down in the bucket. He was now a lot of water that swirled round in the bucket. But, before he could throw himself at Hurry and soak him from head to foot, Hurry caught up the bucket and ran to the well. He tipped up the full bucket – and down into the well went the water, *splishity, splashity, slishity, sloshity*!

Hurry leaned over the well cautiously.

89

Was the goblin powerful enough or clever enough to change back to his own shape again, now that he was in the well? Would he come clambering out, yelling and shouting?

The well-water swirled and splashed, bubbled and gurgled. Then it became quite calm, as it always was. No goblin appeared.

"He's all mixed up with the well-water! He can't find himself! He's split into different drops, and he's got all mixed with the other drops," thought Hurry, gleefully. "He's gone! We've got rid of him! Hurrah! Hurrah! I must go and tell Scurry."

Then he remembered that Scurry was the bucket in his hand. He set it down, and danced round it.

"Dinkle-um-ducket, no longer a bucket. Dinkle-um-durry, come back, dear Scurry!"

The bucket disappeared, and there was Scurry. The two flung themselves at one another. Hurry was almost crying.

"Oh, Scurry, dear Scurry, I'm sorry for

what I did! Oh, Scurry, you carried Crookity, did you know?"

"Yes, I know – and you threw him down the well and he's gone, gone, *gone*," shouted Scurry. "He can't put himself together again. He's all mixed up in the water!"

"I did it all myself! I got rid of him!" sang Hurry. "All by myself I did it."

"You didn't. You couldn't have done it without me!" said Scurry. "If I hadn't been a bucket you couldn't have put him into me when you made him change into water. You didn't do it all by yourself, so there!"

"Don't let's quarrel," said Hurry. "Oh dear, Scurry, do you suppose it's all right to rinse my soapy clothes in well-water now that Crookity's all mixed up in it?"

"I don't know. We'll try," said Scurry, and they raced home to get a bucket. They went to the well, filled it with water, and carried it home between them.

And will you believe it, whenever the well-water is used by anyone for washing, or whenever it is boiled in a kettle, it gurgles and sings in a curious watery voice that says, "Crookity, crookity, crook, crookity, crookity, crook," all the time.

I'd like to hear it – but I don't think I'd much like to use it. I wouldn't be surprised to find the water jumping out of the wash-tub or the kettle, and changing back into the goblin again!

The House Made
of Cards

Wendy and Jack had built a lovely house out of their playing cards. First they put two leaning together, then they put two more on each side, then they put two on top of the side ones resting on them, and built another room on top of that. You know how to do it, don't you?

They made such a big house! Really, they had never made such a large card house before! It was a perfectly lovely one. Wendy called their mother and she cried out in surprise.

"Well, you certainly have built a fine house this time!" she said.

"Could we leave it on the table till the morning?" asked Jack. "It seems a shame to knock it down tonight."

"Well, leave it there," said Mother. "You

can see it tomorrow then. I won't touch it when I lay the table for breakfast."

So the two children left their card house on the table. How big it was!

That night, when all was dark in the room except for the moonlight shining in at the window, a small pixie came hurrying out of a mouse-hole where he had been hiding.

He was looking for a house to live in. He looked into the doll's-house, but the dolls wouldn't let him in.

"We know you, Mister Grabby!" they said. "You'd take the best bed to sleep in, the most comfortable chair to sit in and the nicest cake out of the oven! No, thank you! We don't want you here. Go and look for somewhere else to live!"

Mister Grabby, the pixie, made a rude face at the dolls and wandered off. Then he suddenly saw the lovely house of cards on the table!

"My," he said, "that's a fine house! I wonder if anyone lives there? If nobody does, I shall live there myself! Shan't I be grand! I wonder how many rooms it has?"

He walked into the house of cards. Dear me, it had ten rooms! Would you believe it? Grabby was delighted. He had never had such a grand house before.

He took his tiny magic wand and waved it. He meant to make chairs, tables and beds by magic, and he was just going to utter the right words when he heard a little voice calling to him.

"Mister Grabby! Is this your house?"

Grabby looked out of the top room to see who was speaking. It was the little

95

mouse in whose hole he had been hiding all day.

"Yes, this is my house!" he said grandly. "What do you want?"

"Well, Mister Grabby, that old black cat has come into the house tonight and she's sitting near my hole," said the mouse. "I daren't go back there. So I thought you would perhaps give me shelter in your grand house for tonight."

"I can't," said the selfish pixie. "I want all the rooms myself. I don't want any mice here."

"Oh, Mister Grabby," said the tiny mouse, "how unkind of you! Didn't I share my hole with you when you asked me to yesterday? Please share your house with me till the cat goes away."

"I tell you I won't!" said Grabby crossly. "Go away and be eaten! You're a nuisance!"

Now that made the mouse feel very angry indeed. He made up his mind that he would sleep in the house of cards that night. So he crept in at the bottom of it and lay down to sleep. But the pixie knew

he was there and came flying down in a rage. He hit the mouse with his wand.

"Ow!" cried the mouse and climbed quickly into the room above. The pixie flew after him. Up went the mouse and scrambled into another room. The pixie followed, shouting out in a dreadful temper.

The pixie tried to hit the mouse whenever he could. Soon the tiny creature thought that the pixie was the horridest fellow he had ever met.

"I wish I hadn't shared my hole with you!" he squeaked as he ran in and out of one room after another. "I wish I hadn't! I wish I hadn't!"

Poor little mouse! The pixie caught him at last and hit him on the nose with his magic wand. The little mouse wept tears all down the cards. Then he crept away to the very end of the table and washed his face, thinking hard all the time.

"That pixie wants punishing!" said the mouse. "He's selfish and unkind. I share things with others so why shouldn't he? I shall punish him!"

He watched the pixie climb up into the topmost room of the house of cards. He saw him take a handkerchief out of his pocket to polish up his magic wand.

"I shall go and nibble his house away at the bottom!" said the mouse to himself. "Yes, that's what I will do!"

So, as soon as the pixie had forgotten all about him, he crept back to the house and began to nibble at a card. How he nibbled with his sharp little teeth!

Soon the card was gnawed almost through. It dropped flat on to the table, for it could no longer stand upright! And as soon as it dropped all the house of cards came tumbling down!

Flip, flap, flip, flap! Down it came and

the cards swished softly into a heap on the table. There was no house left. How astonished that pixie was! He had tumbled down with the cards, and bumped his head.

"Oh, oh!" he cried, in a fright. "What is happening? It's an earthquake, it's an earthquake! I must fly away quickly!"

He spread his wings and flew away, quite forgetting to take his little magic wand with him. It lay under the cards. The mouse didn't see it either. He chuckled to himself when he saw what a fright the pixie was in.

"Serves him right!" he said. "And see! The noise of the cards falling has frightened away the cat! I can go back to my hole in safety!"

Back he went, and all was quiet in the room until the children came in the next morning.

"Oh, look!" cried Jack. "Our lovely house of cards has fallen down. And what is this? A card nibbled quite in half! A mouse must have done that – but I wonder why?"

Wendy picked up the cards – and suddenly she found the tiny magic wand.

"Look at this," she said to Jack. "What is it? It looks like a thin silver matchstick with a star at the end!"

"Ooh, it's a magic wand!" said Jack. "Let's use it and see what happens!"

But before they could wish anything their mother called them to go and get ready for school. Wasn't it a pity?

"Never mind, we'll use it tonight after tea!" said Wendy. I do wish I was going to be there, don't you?

Little Marya
and the Witch

Once upon a time there was a little Russian girl called Marya. Her mother was dead, and her father married again, so Marya had a stepmother.

Now, this stepmother did not like Marya, because the child's father was fond of her. So she treated her badly, and made her work very hard.

They lived far away from everybody else on the edge of a great pine forest. The only person who lived at all near to them was a witch who lived in a curious little hut. This hut was perched on one leg, and spun round all day. The witch was not a nice woman, and no one went near her if they could possibly help it.

One day Marya's stepmother said to her, "Marya, I have no buttons to put on your father's new shirt. Run to the witch and ask her to lend me some."

Marya looked at her stepmother in surprise, for she knew that it was dangerous to go near the witch.

"Go quickly," said her stepmother, "or I will beat you, Marya."

Marya did not dare to say she would not go, for she was afraid of being beaten. So she started off with some bread and bacon in a bag, weeping to herself, and wondering what the witch would say when she saw her.

On the way through the forest she met a woodman who looked at her out of kind, wise eyes.

"Why do you weep, little one?" he asked.

"Because I have been sent to the witch," said Marya, "and I am afraid."

"Do not be afraid," said the woodman. "I will help you. Now, listen carefully to me."

Marya listened.

"You will find dogs at the witch's house, who would eat you if they could. Throw them bread to eat and they will leave you alone. There is a cat there too, who would scratch your eyes out if it could. Give it bacon to eat, and it will purr. The door will creak, so oil it well. That is all, Marya. Remember my words, and no harm will come to you."

Marya said thank you to the wise woodman, and went on her way again. Very soon she saw the witch's hut in the distance. It was spinning round and round on its one leg, and looked strange and mysterious. Marya wished she could go home, but she dared not return without the shirt buttons her stepmother wanted.

She went over to the hut, and as she drew near it spun more slowly, and at last stopped. Marya knocked at the door.

"Come in," said a voice.

Marya went in. The witch was sitting at her loom, weaving.

"Good morning," said she. Marya looked at her, and thought she had never seen such an ugly old creature before.

"I have come to borrow some buttons

to sew on my father's shirt," she said timidly.

The witch smiled strangely.

"Wait here while I get them," she said. "Take my place at the loom, and go on with the weaving."

She got up, and Marya sat down in her place. The witch went out of the room and left her alone. She began to cry for she didn't know what was going to happen to her in that odd little hut.

Suddenly she heard a fierce hissing sound, and she saw that a great black cat had come into the room. It was glaring at her, and stretching its claws.

Marya remembered what the wise woodman had said. She quickly undid her little bag and pulled out the piece of bacon she had brought. She threw it to the big cat.

It began purring at once, and ate the bacon hungrily. Then it licked its lips, and looked at Marya.

"Oh, black cat, help me to escape!" cried Marya. "I believe the witch will keep me prisoner and make me her servant."

"That is just what she will do," said
the cat in a deep purring voice. "You must
run off at once while there is a chance.
Stop now and again and lay your ear to
the ground to hear if the witch is coming.
Take this towel and this comb with you,
and if you hear her coming throw down
first the towel, and afterwards the comb.
They will help to save you."

Marya listened, and took the towel and the comb. She thanked the cat, and tiptoed to the door. Then she remembered that the woodman had said it would creak. If it did, perhaps the witch would hear her and come in to stop her going.

She quickly looked round, and on a shelf she saw a can of oil. She took it down and hurriedly oiled the hinges of the door. Then she opened it without a sound and stepped out into a little yard.

Three great dogs were there, and began to growl when they saw her, but she emptied her bag of bread among them and they let her go. Off she ran into the forest, and was soon lost to sight.

The black cat sat down at Marya's place at the loom and began weaving. Presently the witch looked in at the window and called out, "Are you still weaving, Marya?"

The cat pretended to be Marya and answered, "Yes, I am weaving, dear witch!"

The witch knew at once that it was not Marya's voice and she rushed into the hut in a great rage.

"How dare you let that girl escape?"

"She was kind to me," said the cat. "You never gave me anything to eat, but she gave me all her bacon."

Then the witch scolded the door for letting Marya out.

"Haven't I told you that you are only to open inwards and not outwards?" she cried.

"Marya was kind to me," said the door. "She gave my poor, old, creaking hinges oil, and you never once gave me even a drop."

Then the witch went to the dogs and scolded them well.

109

"Haven't I told you never to let anyone go past you!" she stormed.

"Marya was kind to us," they said. "You have given us no food for two days, but Marya gave us all the bread she had."

Then the witch was very angry, and made up her mind to go after Marya and bring her back.

So off she went in her carriage, rumbling quickly along, catching up with Marya.

Marya had run through the forest on her way home, and had already gone a good distance. Suddenly she remembered what the cat had told her to do, so she stopped and put her ear to the ground to see if she could hear the witch coming.

She heard the rumbling of the carriage, and was afraid. Then lo and behold! She saw the witch in the distance, coming nearer and nearer.

Quickly she flung down the towel the cat had given her – and to her enormous surprise it turned into a wide, rushing river.

The witch soon reached it, and looked

at it angrily for it was too wide and deep
to cross. She saw Marya on the other
side, running away as fast as ever she
could.

The witch went back and got ten pairs
of oxen, which she drove to the river
bank. She made them drink all the water
up, but it took a long time, and when at
last she got across, Marya could not be
seen.

The little girl was still a good way from home, though, and after a time she stopped and once more put her ear to the ground and listened. Again she could hear the witch coming nearer. So she took the comb the cat had given her and flung it on the ground.

Lo and behold! It turned into a great tangle of thornwood, so thick and so tall that no one could possibly make their way through it.

When the witch came to it, she tried to force her way into it, but the thorns held

her and scratched, and she had to come out again. Once more she tried, and yet again, and all the time Marya was getting nearer and nearer home.

At last she got so near her home that she could see her stepmother baking bread in the kitchen. But she dared not go into the house, because she had not brought the shirt buttons she had been sent to get.

She sat down outside, wondering what to do, for she was afraid that the witch might come. Just at that moment the wise woodman came through the forest, and saw Marya sitting sadly outside her home.

"You have escaped from the witch then," he said. "That is well done. Tell me about it."

Marya told him.

"But I dare not go home," she said, "because I bring no shirt buttons for my stepmother."

The woodman's face grew stern.

"I will take you in," he said. "You are safe with me, little Marya."

So he put her on his shoulders and carried her indoors. Her stepmother was most surprised to see her. Her father knew nothing of how his little daughter had been sent to the witch, and wondered why the woodman looked so stern.

Then the woodman told of the adventures which Marya had had that day, and how brave she had been. All the time he spoke he looked sternly at the stepmother, till she could bear it no longer.

"I have done wrong," she cried. "Forgive me, husband, and forgive me, Marya. I will be good to you now."

And so she was, and Marya soon grew to love her stepmother, and forgot all about the old witch. When she grew up, the wise woodman came and fetched her to be his wife, and they lived together happily ever after.

As for the witch, she got stuck so fast in the thornwood that she was never able to get out, and there she is to this very day.

Spiny's
Good Turn

Jean loved her little garden. She had two patches. In one she grew flowers and in the other she grew radishes and lettuces for tea.

She really loved taking in a nice fresh lettuce and a dozen radishes to her mother, so that the family could eat them with bread and butter and salt for tea. But this year Jean wasn't having much luck with her garden.

First something ate her seedlings, and she had to plant them again. Then something ate her lettuces.

"I'm afraid it's rabbits, darling," said her mother. "What a nuisance! I don't know why they should choose your bit of garden to nibble at. Never mind – we'll get Daddy to put some wire netting round your two patches, then your plants will be safe."

Well, they were safe from the rabbits – but then something else came to eat the little seedlings and the lettuces, and to gnaw nasty little places in the tender young radishes!

"What is eating my things now?" said Jean, upset. "It's too bad! I'll never be able to bring you flowers or lettuces or radishes this summer, Mummy!"

"It's slugs, dear," said her mother. "And these nasty little caterpillars. You really are unfortunate!"

Now, as Jean went down to her garden the next day, she saw something moving in the hedge. She went to look, and found a little prickly hedgehog caught in a piece of barbed wire there. "Oh dear! Poor little thing," said Jean, "you've hurt your leg!"

She carried the prickly hedgehog in her hanky and went indoors to her mother. They unwrapped it and looked at it. It immediately curled itself up into a tight, spiny ball – but the hurt leg hung out, torn and bleeding.

117

"Poor little creature," said Mother. "I'll put some antiseptic on its leg and bind it up."

So she did. But when it uncurled itself it could hardly walk. "What shall we do with it?" said Jean.

"We must put it somewhere safe for a little while," said her mother. "I know! We'll put it on your garden patch, Jean – the wire netting will keep it safe there till its leg is better. We'll feed it each day."

"Won't it eat my plants?" asked Jean.

"Oh, no. Hedgehogs won't touch those," said Mother. "Look, you carry him there in your hanky, and I'll bring a saucer of food out."

Soon the hedgehog was safely in the wire-enclosed patch. He lay there, curled up tightly, his bandaged leg sticking out of his spines. Jean's mother put down a saucer of dog food. In a few minutes the hedgehog uncurled, smelled the dog food, and dragged himself over to it. He ate it eagerly, taking the pieces into his mouth hungrily.

"I like him," said Jean. "I shall call him Spiny. He's nice. Mummy, look at his funny little snout and his bright, beady eyes. He's looking at me!"

Spiny stayed in the patch for four whole days! He seemed perfectly happy. His leg healed well, and he could soon use it quite easily.

And then Jean noticed something. Her lettuces had grown big and strong. Her radishes were almost ready to eat. Her seedlings hadn't been eaten by slugs or grubs! "How marvellous!" thought Jean.

"Mummy – it's Spiny that has eaten up every grub and caterpillar and slug!" she said, in surprise. "I watched him today, snuffling under a lettuce – and he brought out a big, fat slug and gobbled it up!"

"Well, fancy even a little hedgehog repaying a good turn!" said Mother. "Who would have thought it?"

Jean was quite right. The hedgehog had looked for grubs and caterpillars and had gobbled up every one he found! No wonder the lettuces and radishes grew well.

"I do wish Spiny would stay in our garden," said Jean. "He would be so useful. I'd like to have a hedgehog for a pet. But I expect he'll wander away as soon as I set him free."

"Well, he can't stay in your little wired-up patch now that his leg is better," said her mother. "He's a wild animal and we must set him free."

So they set him free – but do you know, Spiny didn't wander away! He liked Jean and he liked the garden. So he stayed, and made himself into a pet. How do I know all this?

Well, you see, I went to tea with Jean the other day and had fine red radishes and crisp green lettuce out of her garden. She told me about Spiny, of course, and I went to see him. Isn't she lucky to have a hedgehog to eat all her slugs?

The Beautiful
Toy Duck

Mollie had the finest toy duck you ever saw. It came from America, from her rich Auntie Sadie, and it was almost exactly like a real duckling!

It was bigger than a duckling. It was covered with yellow down and yellow feathers. It had a fine duck-beak, a waggly tail, and two big webbed feet, just like those of a real duck.

And do you know, it quacked! When Mollie pulled one of its legs very gently it said "Quack! Quack!" It made everyone jump when they heard it, because it sounded so very real.

"It's a beautiful toy," said her mother. "Too expensive and too beautiful to be played with carelessly, Mollie. Wouldn't you like to keep it for special days –

Sundays, say – and only have it out then?"

"Oh, no, Mummy!" said Mollie. "It's no fun having a toy I can't show to everyone. Let me play with it every day. I promise to be very, very careful."

"Well, don't take it out into the garden," said her mother. "It would be dreadful if you left it out in the rain, as you left Rosebud one day."

The duck was called Quack. He was a merry-looking toy, soft and cuddly, and Mollie took him up to bed with her every night. She really loved him. Quack went

everywhere with Mollie; out shopping, out to tea. He stood on the table at meal-times, and watched out of his bright glass eyes.

One morning Mollie went into the garden to play. Somebody called to her over the wall. "Mollie! Have you got your duck? I've got my cousin staying with me and he would so like to see it."

Mollie forgot that her mother said she mustn't take the duck into the garden. She sped into the house to get it. Soon she was showing it to Sue and Harry, and they cried out in delight when she pulled the duck's leg and it quacked.

Their dog looked at it in wonder. A duck! Yet it didn't smell like the ducks on the pond at the farm. He tried to sniff at it, but the children wouldn't let him.

"No, Scamp, no! You're not to go near it! You might nibble it." Scamp cocked his ears up every time the duck quacked. He couldn't understand it at all.

"Mollie, climb over and see the lovely tent we've got," said Sue. "It's under the cherry trees."

Mollie put the duck carefully down on the garden seat. Then she climbed over the wall to see the lovely tent.

She stayed quite a long time and had some fine games with Harry and Sue. Then she climbed back over the wall. She remembered her duck on the seat, and went to get it.

But it wasn't there! It was gone. Mollie stared at the empty garden seat in dismay. She looked all round and about, but there was no yellow duckling anywhere. She rushed indoors, crying.

"Mummy! Have you taken my duck? It's gone!"

"No, of course I haven't," said her mother. "Isn't it in your room? Where did you put it?"

Mollie went red. "Oh, dear! I took it out into the garden, and you told me not to. I wanted to show it to Sue and Harry. I put it on the garden seat – and now it's gone!"

Mollie wailed loudly. "Somebody's stolen it! And I did love it so."

"Oh, Mollie – something always happens when you are disobedient," said Mother. "That really was naughty of you. You will be so upset if someone really has stolen the duck."

Well, nobody could find that duck, though everyone hunted hard, Sue and Harry, too. It simply wasn't anywhere to be found. Mollie wouldn't eat any lunch, she was so upset.

She went out into the garden before tea to have one last look. And then she heard a little noise that made her jump.

"Quack! Quack!"

"My duck!" cried Mollie. "Where is it?" She listened again, and then, sure enough, she heard the little quacking. It came from the garden next door.

In a trice Mollie was over the wall. "Quack, quack." There it was again. She ran towards the noise and came to Scamp's kennel. The noise came from there! Quack must be calling for help.

Mollie crawled into Scamp's kennel. Scamp was there, lying on his blanket. Beside him was Quack, his feathers damp with being licked. "Quack!" he said.

"Oh, Scamp! You bad, naughty dog! You must have slipped into my garden and taken Quack off the seat!" scolded Mollie. "Poor, poor Quack! Have you hurt him?"

No, Quack wasn't hurt at all. Scamp hadn't even given him a gentle nibble.

He had licked him well, that was all, so that all his fluffiness had gone.

Mollie took him back to her mother. "I've found Quack!" she said. "Scamp had him in his kennel, the bad dog. Oh, Mummy, will Quack's fluffiness come back?"

"Oh, yes," said Mollie's mother. "I'll rub him over with a wet sponge to wipe away Scamp's licks, and then we'll put him in the sun to dry. But it wasn't Scamp who was to blame for Quack being lost, Mollie, was it?"

"No. It really was my fault," said Mollie. "I'm sorry, Mummy. I'll remember what you say another time. Oh, Mummy, wasn't Quack clever, quacking for help like that? That's how I found him, you know. I heard him call 'Quack, quack, quack!'"

"Oh, that was just Scamp pulling the duck's leg and making him quack," said Mother.

But Mollie didn't think so. What do you think?

Mister Wiggle's Scissors

Mister Wiggle was a tailor who made a lot of money. He lived in Fiddle-Town, and he owned a marvellous pair of scissors that people came miles to see.

These scissors were made of pure gold, and had a magic spell in them. Wiggle had only to put them down on a piece of cloth and say "Scissors, cut out a dress" or "Scissors, cut out a fine pair of trousers" and at once the golden scissors would set to work. They saved Mister Wiggle a lot of time and trouble besides giving him a great name for wonderful dress and tunic patterns.

Even the Queen of Fairyland had been known to order a special dress from him. But Wiggle wasn't at all vain. He lived in his little cottage and worked hard week in and week out. There was just one thing he wanted and had never had – and that was a chance to be the chief brownie in Fiddle-Town and sit on the silver chair at all the town meetings.

But only clever brownies were allowed to do that, and although Wiggle was really a very thoughtful, wise brownie, he was so quiet that no one really thought of him as clever, and he was never voted for when a new chief brownie had to be chosen.

Now one day a strange piece of news went round Fiddle-Town. There was an empty house at the end of the village, and someone had taken it to live in and that someone was a witch! A witch in

Fiddle-Town! That really was a most extraordinary thing, for witches did not usually come to live near brownies. Brownies hated witches and feared them.

This witch was well known. Her name was Greeneye and you can guess why. She was a wicked, sly creature, always making up strange, cunning magic. She had been banished from the last town she had lived in, and when she heard of the empty house in Fiddle-Town she thought it would suit her well, and moved in the very next day.

"What are we going to do about Witch Greeneye?" asked the brownies at their next meeting. Mister Heyho, the chief brownie, sat in the silver chair and looked solemnly at everyone. Really, something would have to be done, he said. But nobody knew what!

"Well," said Heyho, rising from his silver chair, "if anyone thinks of a really good idea he had better be the next chief brownie, because I can't think of anything!"

Mister Wiggle the tailor went home

and thought hard. Here was a chance for him to be chief – if only he could think of a good idea. He sat down in his rocking-chair and thought for quite twenty minutes. And at the end of that time he smiled. He had thought of a plan.

His windows looked out on the back garden of the witch's house. Wiggle watched to see when the witch had her washing-day. On the next Tuesday he saw a great many clothes hanging out on the line.

He quickly put on his hat and went to call on the West Wind, who was a great friend of his.

"West Wind," he said, "will you do me a favour? There's a nasty old witch living just near my house and she has hung all her washing out on her line. Would you please go along and blow it all away and hide it for a little while where she can't find it?"

"But what for?" asked West Wind, in surprise.

"Never mind what for," answered Wiggle. "I've got a very good reason."

"Very well," said the wind, laughing. "It will be a good joke. I'll go along and do it now."

So when Greeneye the witch looked out of her kitchen window to see how her clothes were drying, she got a terrible shock – for West Wind had just that very minute blown along, and was sweeping every single one of her nicely washed clothes off the line.

Away they went, two dresses and two cloaks, three petticoats and a veil. West

Wind blew them up the hill and down the other side. Greeneye raced after them, but when she got to the top they were nowhere to be seen. West Wind had hidden them away very cunningly.

"Oh, you villain," cried Greeneye to the wind. "You've stolen away all my clothes! Now I shall have to go and buy some more!"

That was just what Mister Wiggle the tailor wanted. He peeped through his window and was delighted to see the

135

witch walking towards his shop. Soon she had opened the door and walked in.

"Hello, Mister Wiggle," she called banging on the counter. "Where are you? Don't keep me waiting."

"Sorry," said Wiggle, coming out of his workshop. "I'm very busy, just at the moment!"

"Well, you may be busy, but you've got to put all your other work on one side and make me some dresses and a cloak," snapped the witch. "That wretched West

Wind has stolen all the clothes off my line, and I must have some more. I want them by tomorrow."

"I'm afraid that's impossible," said Wiggle, politely. "I've a tunic to finish for Heyho, the chief brownie, and a gown for Mrs Tiddlywinks, and a pair of trousers for her little boy."

"Don't be silly," said the witch, sharply. "You must put everything on one side and make what I want! You don't want me to turn you into a black beetle for disobeying me, do you?"

"No, I don't," said Wiggle, pretending to be frightened. "But I really must finish these jobs first, Witch Greeneye. But I have an idea – perhaps if I lent you my magic scissors you could get them to cut out what you want, and then sew the things together yourself. It's the cutting out that is so difficult, isn't it? But if you had my scissors, you could easily get them to do the hard part for you, and then it wouldn't cost you much to have the things you want – you could just sew up the seams yourself."

"That's a good idea," said the witch, who was always pleased to save money when she could. "Where are these scissors?"

"I'll go and get them," said Wiggle, and he went into his workshop, grinning to himself. He picked up his golden scissors, and took half the spell out of them before he gave them to the witch. She didn't wait to thank him but went straight off to her house with them, planning all the dresses she would have.

She pulled some material from a box and spread it out on the table. Then she popped the scissors on it and commanded them to set to work. In a trice they opened themselves and began to cut the cloth out in the shape of a dress. The witch was delighted.

She laid out another piece of cloth and the scissors cut out a cloak for her. Then she thought she would sew up the dress and the cloak, and she put the scissors on her kitchen dresser. But how great was her surprise to hear them still clipping merrily away! She looked up and saw

138

that they had jumped to the curtains and were busily cutting them out in the shape of a coat!

"You wicked things! Stop that at once," cried the witch, in a rage. She caught hold of the scissors, but let them go with a shout for they quickly pricked her hand with their points. They flew to the tablecloth and began to cut it up in the shape of a pair of trousers. The witch was so angry that she hardly knew what to do.

She did not dare to touch the scissors again, but she quickly looked up all her magic books to see what words she should use to make them stop. But she could find nothing at all to help her. It was dreadful.

The scissors cut up the carpet next and then all the cushions in the chairs. Then they neatly cut up the kettle-holder and flew into the bedroom to see what they could do to the bedspread and sheets!

The witch followed them, shouting and crying with rage, but it wasn't a bit of good. She simply could not stop those scissors! And, oh dear me, when they had finished cutting up everything they could, what do you think they did? They flew to the witch herself, and began to cut off her hair! Then they started to cut her clothes into rags, and poor Greeneye rushed out of the house in terror.

She ran to Mister Wiggle's and burst into his shop with the scissors busily cutting the laces of her boots.

"Mister Wiggle! What's wrong with these scissors? They won't stop cutting!

Put the right spell into them at once, or I will turn you into an earwig."

"Well, if you turn me into an earwig, those scissors will never leave you!" said Wiggle, sewing busily at a coat. "Now, Witch Greeneye, let us talk together. I will tell you truthfully that I have taken half the spell from my scissors – and I don't mean to put it back again until you promise me something."

"You wicked brownie! What do you want me to promise you?"

"You must promise me to pack your box and leave Fiddle-Town for ever," said Wiggle, sewing on a button at top speed.

141

"We don't like you. You're cunning and sly. We would much rather have your room than your company."

"Well, I shall stay!" shouted the witch in a terrible temper. "I shall stay – and I shall make all sorts of terrible spells to punish you and the other brownies!"

"Well, the scissors will stay too," said Wiggle. "Be careful they don't cut off your nose. I see they've cut off your hair already."

"Oh! Oh! Oh!" wailed the witch. "What shall I do? Go away, you hateful scissors! Stop cutting, I tell you!"

But the scissors took not the slightest notice, and managed to snip off the toes of both her boots.

Suddenly Greeneye boxed Mister Wiggle's ear hard and ran out of his shop, the scissors following her. She went weeping to her house and packed all her things into three big boxes. Then she clapped her hands seven times and four broomsticks came flying through the air. The witch tied a box on each of the three biggest, and then sat herself on the

143

smallest, with her big black cat behind her.

"Away! Away!" she cried. At once the broomsticks rose up into the air and Wiggle ran out to call all the brownies of Fiddle-Town to see the wonderful sight of Witch Greeneye really leaving the village at last.

"Hurrah! Hurrah!" they cried. "How did you make her go, Mister Wiggle?"

"Come here, scissors!" shouted Wiggle. He was afraid that his magic scissors might follow the witch in her travels. The scissors flew down into his hand and he shut them. They stayed still and cut no more until he next commanded them. He knew the magic word to halt them in their work.

Wiggle told all the brownies what he had done, and called West Wind to ask him where he had hidden the witch's clothes. The West Wind blew them out of a cave on the other side of the hill. Wiggle packed them into a basket and bade the wind blow them after the witch.

"We don't want anything belonging to

such a cunning creature left behind," he said. "Well, fellow brownies, I hope you approve of what I have done for you."

"Clever old Wiggle!" shouted everyone, and they hoisted him up on their shoulders. "You shall sit in the silver chair and be our chief brownie! Clever old Wiggle!"

Mister Wiggle was delighted. He sat down in the silver chair and beamed at everyone. It was the very proudest day of his life.

145

"Scissors, you must share my glory," he said, and he took them from his pocket and set them on the seat beside him. Then everyone cheered madly, and the scissors were so alarmed that they jumped back into their master's pocket again.

No one knows what became of Witch Greeneye. It is said that her broomstick bumped into a thunderbolt and disappeared. It is certain that she was never seen again!

Sally
Suck-a-Thumb

Once there was a little girl called Sally Suck-a-Thumb! Guess why! Well, you guessed right if you said it was because she would keep sucking her thumb.

You know, some children suck their thumbs when they are little and some don't. Sometimes they suck their thumbs because they are lonely or unhappy, and sometimes just because it's a habit they can't get out of.

Well, Sally wasn't lonely and she wasn't unhappy either. She was just an ordinary, cheerful little girl with plenty of toys and friends – and a thumb she sucked half the night and half the day!

"Don't be such a baby, Sally," said her mother. "Babies suck their thumbs! You are a big girl."

Sally took her thumb out of her mouth. In half a minute it was in again! You see, she just couldn't remember.

"You know, Sally," said Granny, "you are growing your nice new teeth in front – your second, grown-up teeth. If you keep putting your thumb in your mouth to suck, it will push your growing teeth outwards, and you will have rabbit-teeth, sticking out over your lip. You wouldn't like that, would you?"

"No," said Sally, and she took her thumb out of her mouth at once. But in half a minute it was in again! Poor Sally Suck-a-Thumb! How she wished she could remember not to suck that little pink thumb.

Sally was a kind girl. She was always doing nice things for people, and one day she did something kind for a funny old lady she met down Cuckoo Lane.

Sally didn't know that the old lady was half a fairy, because, except for her bright green eyes, she looked just like any other old lady.

She was carrying a big basket of all

kinds of things, and suddenly a cow behind the hedge mooed very loudly indeed. The old lady had a fright, tipped up her basket, and out fell all the things she had bought!

"Oh dear, oh dear!" she said. "Look at that! I must pick them up again, and I do find it so hard to bend down now I'm old and stiff."

Sally saw and heard all this and she ran up at once. "I'll pick everything up for you," she said. "I'd love to."

She picked up the butter. She picked up the tea and the sugar. She found where all

the potatoes had rolled to. She discovered a tin of polish lying under a clump of nettles, and had to let her hand get stung by them when she picked it up.

"Oh, you're stung!" cried the old lady. "Let me see."

Sally held up her hand. The old lady looked at it. "Was it your thumb that got stung?" she asked. "It looks rather red and sore."

"No; that's only because I'm always sucking it," said Sally. "I love sucking my thumb, you know."

"How funny!" said the old lady. "I would much rather suck toffee, or something like that."

"Oh, well, so would I," said Sally. "Though my favourite sweet is peppermint rock. You know – the kind you get at the seaside. I simply love that."

"Do you really?" said the old lady. "Well, in return for your kindness, little girl, I'll do something for you – you shall have peppermint rock to suck all day long and all night long, if you want to!"

"Oh, thank you," said Sally, thinking

that the old lady meant to give her some. But she didn't, and walked off down the lane.

Sally stared after her. What did she mean about having peppermint rock to suck all day long and all night long? The little girl popped her thumb into her mouth as usual and thought hard.

And, dear me, what a very, very extraordinary thing – her thumb tasted of peppermint rock!

Sally could hardly believe it. She took her thumb out of her mouth and looked at it – and, do you know, it had gone that funny reddish-pink colour that all peppermint rock is, on the outside.

151

"I do believe my thumb is made of peppermint rock!" said Sally in the greatest surprise. She popped it into her mouth again. Yes – the more she sucked her thumb the more she tasted peppermint rock. How very, very nice!

She ran home to tell her mother. Her mother couldn't believe that such a funny thing had happened, but when she tasted Sally's thumb herself she found that the little girl was right – it *was* made of peppermint rock!

But then Sally's mother looked very serious and solemn. "If it's peppermint rock," she said, "you will suck it all away, Sally! You know sweets don't last for ever! What will you do without a thumb?"

Sally stared at her mother in dismay! Good gracious! She hadn't thought of that! She popped her thumb into her mouth as she always did when she thought hard. But at once she took it out again. This would never do! She must *not* suck away her nice, useful little thumb!

"Oh, Mummy! The old lady thought she was doing me a good turn, but she wasn't," said Sally, half crying. "She forgot I might suck my thumb away! Already I think I've sucked it thinner since it became peppermint rock."

"Well, darling, for goodness' sake do remember not to suck it any more," her mother said anxiously. "And as soon as you see the old lady again, tell her she did you a bad turn, not a good turn, and ask her to take away your peppermint thumb and let you have your own proper one."

But, you know, Sally didn't see the old lady for weeks and weeks, though she looked for her every day. And all that while Sally didn't suck her thumb, because as soon as she popped it into her mouth the taste of peppermint reminded her that she might suck her thumb right away – and she took it out at once.

So, by the time she did see the old lady again, Sally no longer sucked her thumb! She had quite got out of the habit, and people didn't call her Sally Suck-a-Thumb any more. Sally was very glad.

And then, one Friday, she met the old lady in the lane. She knew her at once because of her very green eyes. Sally ran up to her.

"Good morning!" she said. "Do you remember me? You said you would do me a good turn and you gave me a peppermint thumb to suck – but it was really a very bad turn because I might have sucked my thumb all away!"

"My dear little girl!" said the old lady, her green eyes shining kindly, "you are wrong. I did you a good turn by giving you a peppermint thumb – because, you see, I knew you would be sensible enough not to suck it – and so you would quite get out of the habit by the time I next saw you! I am sure I am right."

"Well – you are!" said Sally in surprise. "I don't suck my thumb any more – I don't even want to – so you have cured me of the habit. Please let me have my own proper thumb again, for I know I shall never suck it any more."

"Very well," said the old lady. "Have your own proper little thumb – but, Sally, if ever you do begin to suck it again, you will taste peppermint, and that will warn you to take it out at once!"

Sally looked down at her thumb – it

was pale pink again, soft and warm – not a peppermint-rock thumb any longer. How glad she was! She looked up to thank the old lady, but she was gone. Sally ran home to her mother.

"The old lady did me a good turn after all!" she cried, and she told her mother what had happened. "I'm cured, Mummy, and I'm so glad."

She was cured – but once, when she put her thumb in her mouth to suck a thorn out, what do you suppose she tasted? Yes – peppermint! Wasn't it strange?

The Ball
That Vanished

Jenny and Adam had a beautiful big rubber ball. It was bright blue one side and bright red the other side, and when it rolled along quickly it wasn't blue or red, but purple instead.

"It goes purple when it rolls because the blue and the red mix up together and make purple!" said Jenny, who knew quite a lot about painting.

They played every day with the big blue and red ball. They rolled it, they kicked it, they threw it, they bounced it. It didn't mind a bit what they did with it. It just loved everything.

And then one day it vanished. It really was rather extraordinary, because neither Jenny nor Adam saw where it went.

They were having a fine game of throw-the-ball-over-the-house. I don't know whether you have ever played that game, but if your house isn't too high it is rather fun. One of you stands at the front of the house, and the other one stands at the back, and you can only do it if Mother says you may. Anyway, Mother said that Adam and Jenny might play it till teatime.

So Adam stood at the back and Jenny stood at the front. Adam threw the ball high into the air and it went right over the house. Jenny saw it coming over the chimney and she gave a shout of joy. She held out her hands for it, and it dived right down into them.

"I've caught it, Adam!" she cried. "Look out – it's coming back to you!"

She threw it up into the air – but she didn't throw it hard enough and it struck the tiles, rolled down the roof, and fell back into her hands again. She threw it once more, and this time it sailed right over the top. Adam gave a shout.

"I see it! It's coming! Good throw, Jenny. I've caught it!"

Then Adam aimed the ball high again and up it went over the house once more. But Jenny didn't call out that she could see it coming. There was no sound from her at all.

"Jenny! Have you caught it?" shouted Adam.

"No. It hasn't come over yet," said Jenny, puzzled. "Did you throw it? Did it go right over the roof?"

"Of course," said Adam. "Didn't you

hear me shout when I threw it? It must have fallen somewhere on your side, Jenny. You'll have to look for it."

So Jenny looked all over the front garden, but not a sign of that big blue and red ball did she see. It was most annoying. Adam came running round to the front.

"Haven't you found it yet?" he asked. "Jenny, you don't know how to look!"

"I do!" said Jenny crossly. "I've looked everywhere. It's you that doesn't know how to throw! The ball must have fallen back into your half of the garden. I shall go and look there!"

So Adam hunted in the front garden and Jenny hunted in the back one. But neither of them could find that ball. It really had completely vanished. It was very odd. They went in and told Mother.

"Could a ball disappear into the air?" asked Adam.

"Of course not," said his mother. "It's a pity if you have lost that nice ball. It really was a beauty."

Well, that wasn't the only unpleasant

thing to happen that day. When the children went to their toy cupboard to look for another toy to play with, they found the room full of smoke.

"Mummy, Mummy, the house is on fire!" said silly Jenny, with a scream. But Adam knew better.

"It's the chimney smoking!" he cried. "Mummy, come and put the fire out in the grate. The smoke is coming out into the room."

Mother hurried in, vexed and worried. How she did hate to see all the smoke pouring out into the room and making it black and dirty!

161

"I can't imagine why it is doing this," she said, vexed. "The sweep only came a few weeks ago. Oh dear – it's no good, I must ring him up and tell him to come. Some damp soot must have stopped up the chimney."

So the sweep came with his brushes, and the children watched him in delight. Sweeping a chimney seemed a most glorious thing to do, and both Jenny and Adam made up their minds that when they were grown-up they would spend at any rate a little time of their lives being chimney-sweeps.

The sweep put a brush up the chimney, and then fitted another pole to the brush-handle. He pushed that up the chimney too. Then he fitted on another pole and pushed that up as well.

"You see, Jenny, all these long poles push the brush higher and higher up the chimney, sweeping as it goes, till it comes to the top!" said Adam, in delight.

"Does the brush come right out of the top of the chimney?" asked Jenny.

"Of course," said the sweep, his black face smiling at them, showing very white teeth. "You run outside into the garden, Missy, and shout to me when you see my old black brush poking itself out of the top of your chimney. Then I'll know it is right out and I won't fit on any more poles."

So out went Adam and Jenny and watched the chimney. And soon Jenny gave a scream of joy.

"Look, Adam, look! The brush is just coming out!"

Sure enough, something was coming out of the chimney. It was the sweep's brush – but on top of it was something round and black and strange. Whatever could it be?

"What's that on top of the brush?" said Adam. "Is it a black stone, do you think? I'll go and tell the sweep."

So into the house he ran and told the surprised sweep that there was something on top of his brush.

"A bird's nest, maybe," said the sweep. "Birds sometimes build their nests in a chimney, you know, and that stops it up, and makes it smoke. I'll come and look."

So the sweep left his long poles standing upright in the grate, and went out to look. He stared and stared at the thing on top of his round brush, and then he went back indoors again.

"I'll shake and wriggle my poles so that the brush throws off that thing, whatever it is," he said. "I really don't know what it can be."

So he shook his poles and the brush shook too – and off came that round black thing, bounced all the way down the roof and fell into the garden!

And it was – yes – you've all guessed

right! It was the children's big ball, very black, very sooty, and very sorry for itself indeed!

"Oh! It's our ball!" shouted Adam, picking it up and making his hands all sooty. "Oh, Jenny – it fell down the chimney when I threw it up! And it stopped up the chimney and made it smoke! It must just have fitted the chimney pot!"

Jenny was excited and pleased. "Let's

wash it," she said. "Won't Mummy be surprised!"

So they washed the ball, and it came all clean and blue and red again. But it never bounced quite so high as it once used to, because the chimney had been hot, and the ball had been nearly cooked.

And now the children don't like to play throw-the-ball-over-the-house in case it pops down the chimney again! Mother says it really costs her too much to look after a ball that is so fond of chimneys!

The Bunny on
the Birthday Cake

There was once a little girl whose pet
name was Bunny. She was soft and
cuddlesome, and she had brown hair and
brown eyes, and looked a little bit like a
cuddly rabbit. So everyone called her
Bunny.

When she was seven years old her
mother made her a birthday cake. You
should have seen it! It had pink and white
icing, seven pink and white candles in a
ring, candied violets round the edge, and
silver balls everywhere.

And in the very middle was a white
bunny, holding a little card that said
"Many happy returns of the day".

"Oh, Mummy!" cried Bunny, in delight.
"What a lovely cake. I do like it. And it's
got a white bunny in the middle to hold

the card! It's a proper bunny birthday cake for me."

The white bunny in the middle of the cake was very proud to be there. He squatted on his hind legs, holding the card in one of his paws, his long ears cocked upwards. "I'm the bunny on the birthday cake," he told the toys when they came climbing up on to the table to see him the night before the birthday. "I'm the bunny on the birthday cake. I'm grand. I'm important. I'm in the very, very middle of the cake, in the very, very middle of the table."

"Ho!" said the bear, who felt a bit jealous. "And very soon you'll be in the very, very middle of all the children!"

"What do you mean?" said the white bunny in alarm.

"You'll be eaten!" said the bear. "That's what I mean. You're a sugar bunny, meant to be eaten. They'll bite off your ears, and your little bobtail, they'll chew up your legs and that will be the end of you."

"I don't want to be eaten! I don't want to be chewed," wailed the white rabbit. "I don't want there to be an end of me. I want to go on and on, like you toys do. I don't want to be eaten."

"Well, you will be," said the bear. "On the last birthday cake there was a tree all made of sugar, and that was eaten. And on the Christmas cake there was a sugar Father Christmas, and he was eaten too. So you are sure to be."

"I shall run away," said the bunny. "I shall hop off the cake and hide. I shall, I shall."

"I thought you were so proud of being

on the birthday cake," said the bear. "Now you want to run away. You are a coward!"

"If you do run away, the little girl called Bunny, whose cake it is, will be very, very sad," said the big doll. "The birthday cake won't be nearly so lovely without you. Still – run away if you like."

"Shh! There's someone coming," said the bear, suddenly. The toys climbed down quickly and ran to the toy cupboard. When Bunny's father came into the room to look at the cake there was no toy to be seen. Only the little white bunny on the cake stared at Father with scared eyes. Oh dear, oh dear – he was going to be eaten! Sugar bunnies always were eaten!

When Father went the little white bunny wondered whether to run away or not. He could jump off the cake and go down a mouse-hole. It would be very easy.

"But the little girl will cry if I am not here on her cake," thought the bunny. "It's her birthday tomorrow. I don't want to make her unhappy. I'd better stay."

So, although he was dreadfully afraid of

being eaten the very next day, he stayed on the cake. There he sat, all night long, holding the little birthday card, thinking in fright of the next day.

The next morning came, and the afternoon came. Bunny was having a party, and at three o'clock all the boys and girls trooped in at the front door. At four o'clock they all came into the dining-room to have tea – and there was the wonderful birthday cake on the table, its seven candles waiting to be lit, and the little white bunny sitting in the very middle.

"How lovely! Oh, how lovely! Look at the bunny! Isn't he sweet? Oh, how wonderful!" cried the children, in joy.

They ate the sandwiches. They ate the biscuits and buns. Then the candles were lit on the birthday cake, and they shone on the little white rabbit.

"He looks a bit scared," said Bunny, staring at him. "Isn't he sweet?"

"Can we all have a bit of him?" asked Mary, eagerly. "When we've had a slice of the cake, can we have a nibble at the bunny?"

The bunny trembled. He shivered so much that the card fell out of his paw. Oh, why hadn't he run away when he had had the chance?

"I don't think I want to eat him," said Bunny. "He looks so sweet."

"Oh, we must, we must!" cried Mary. "I'd like to nibble his ears!"

"Well, dears, I'm afraid you won't be able to eat the little white bunny," said Mother, with a laugh. "You see, he isn't made of sugar, though he looks like it. He is made of china. So he can't possibly be eaten. He will stand on Bunny's windowsill when the cake is finished, and look quite sweet there for a long, long time!"

Well, wasn't the little white bunny glad when he heard that! He almost galloped round the cake! As it was, he flicked his ears, and Bunny was sure she saw him.

"He's glad, he's glad!" she said. "He didn't want to be eaten. And now he won't be."

How glad he was that he hadn't run away and lived down a dirty, smelly mouse-hole. Now he sits on Bunny's windowsill, next to the clock, and watches everything that goes on. Bunny loves him and so would you if you saw him. Perhaps you will some day.

Ben's Forgettery

"I don't know what is the matter with you lately, Ben," said his mother. "Your memory is so very, very bad! Whatever I ask you to do, you forget!"

"He's got a forgettery, Mummy, not a memory," said Bella, with a giggle.

"No, I haven't!" said Ben, crossly. "I can remember anything if I really try to."

"That's the whole point," said his mother. "You don't try to."

"I'll remember the very next thing you tell me to do, just see if I don't!" said Ben.

Well, the next morning, as the twins were setting off to school, Mother gave Ben a big, square letter to post. "Now don't forget!" she said. "Daddy specially wants this letter to catch the early post."

"Right," said Ben. "Look, Mum, I'll carry it in my hand with my dictation book. I promise I won't forget to post it."

He and Bella went off to school, hopping and skipping about as they always did. They went right past the pillar-box, of course, before Ben remembered the letter.

"I'm going back to post it!" he shouted

to Bella, and back he went. He ran to catch up Bella, and they soon got to school.

The first lesson was dictation. Bella put her book on her desk – and Ben was just going to do the same when he got a dreadful shock!

It wasn't his dictation book in his hand. It was Daddy's big, square letter!

"Oh! Bella, I've posted my dictation book instead of Daddy's letter!" said Ben. He put up his hand. "Please, Miss Brown, I've posted my dictation book by mistake, instead of this letter. May I go and post it now?"

"Certainly not!" said Miss Brown. "And you must buy a new dictation book with your own money, Ben. You have been getting really very careless lately."

"Oh dear – what will Daddy say when he knows I've missed the post!' groaned Ben.

"I expect he'll say quite a lot," said Bella. And she was right!

The
Magic Seaweed

One day Jill was building a sandcastle by the sea. It was a lovely one with passages here and there through it, and a proper tower at the top with windows to look through, and a nice courtyard paved with little white stones.

All round the castle was a moat that Jill had dug herself. She fetched some water from the sea to fill it, but the water sank down through the sand and the moat stayed dry.

"Never mind!" said her mother, who was sitting near by, reading. "When the tide comes in, it will fill your moat and then the castle will look lovely, all surrounded by blue water!"

Jill finished the castle and then sat down to wait for the tide. She picked up a bit of red seaweed lying on the sand near her and began to pop the little bladders in it, one by one.

Suddenly she came to an oddly-shaped little bladder, and she popped it just as she had done the others – and inside she found a little pink sweet! Jill looked at it in astonishment.

It certainly looked like a sweet – but did it taste like one? Jill popped it into her mouth to see. Yes, it was lovely and sweet and tasted of strawberries!

The little girl sucked till it was gone – and then she saw that a very strange thing had happened. She had grown quite small! She wasn't even as tall as her little pail lying near by!

"Goodness, that seaweed must be magic!" said Jill. "I've gone small. Oh my, doesn't Mummy look big! She's just like a giantess!"

Jill looked at her sandcastle. It looked very, very big to her now, and she thought she would like to explore it. She ran across the dry moat and climbed up the little sandy steps she had made in the side of the castle and went inside.

It was all very exciting. She ran down one of the passages, and was surprised to hear someone speaking to her.

"Hello, pixie! Where did you come from?"

Jill turned and saw a crab as big as herself. She felt a little bit afraid at first, but the crab looked at her kindly, and she thought that he looked too nice to nip her.

"I'm not a pixie," she said. "I'm just a little girl gone very small. I ate a magic sweet out of one of those bladders in the seaweed."

"Dear me, that's very interesting," said the crab, crawling out of the damp corner

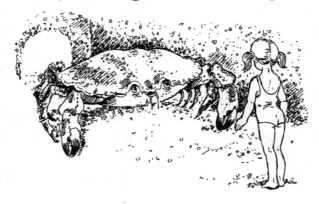

179

he was hiding in. "Have you come to live here?"

"Oh no," said Jill. "I've only come to explore. I built this castle when I was big, you know."

"Very clever of you," said the crab. "But how are you going to get out again? The tide is coming in, and soon the castle will be surrounded by water!"

"Oh, goodness me, I'd better go quickly then," said Jill, in a fright. "I never thought of that."

She turned and ran down the passage to the sandy steps that led to the moat. But when she got to the moat she stood still and stared.

A big wave had swept up the sand and had filled the moat all round the castle! Water rippled against the sandy walls, and now that Jill was so tiny, she knew she could not possibly wade through it. It was much too deep!

"Whatever shall I do?" she said. "Perhaps Mummy will hear me if I shout, and lift me off."

So she shouted to her mother at the

top of her voice. But Mother didn't hear at all. The sea was making such a noise and Jill's voice was now so small that she could hardly hear it herself!

"Well, Mummy can't hear me, that's certain," said Jill. "I'll go back to the crab and see what he's going to do. He's here too."

So she went back to him and asked him.

"That's easy," said the crab. "I shall wait until the castle crumbles right away into the sea and then swim down to the sandy bottom and bury myself there! Why don't you do the same?"

"Little girls don't do things like that," said Jill. "Oh dear, whatever shall I do?

181

Look, there's another big wave gone by and filled the moat up again. And, oh dear, it has washed away my nice sandy steps up to this passage. Perhaps the next one will come into this very passage, Mister Crab! I'm going up to the top of the castle. I shall feel safer there!"

She ran out of the passage and climbed up the side of the castle till she came to the little doorway she had made in the castle walls at the top. She slipped through it and found herself in the courtyard of white pebbles. They seemed very big to her now. She ran to a window and looked out. Oh my goodness, the sea was certainly coming in fast!

"It will be all round the castle in a minute!" she thought. "Look at that enormous wave!"

Smack! The wave broke just near the castle, and the sea ran all round it. There was no moat to be seen now, for the tide had quite surrounded the castle. Jill could see nothing but green sea all around.

Smack! Another big wave broke, and Jill felt the castle shake beneath her.

"The castle will soon be gone," said the crab, suddenly appearing through the doorway. "It doesn't take long for the sea to destroy a building made of sand, you know."

"But this is dreadful!" cried Jill, in a great fright. "Why, I might be drowned! Oh, do look at the next wave!"

Smack! The wave broke so far up the castle that all the front side of it crumbled

183

down into the sea! Only the back of it stood above the water, and poor Jill clambered to the very highest piece. Oh dear! What a tiny island she was on, and what a big sea was all around her! Her mother had moved further up the beach, out of the reach of the water. She didn't seem to miss Jill at all.

"Mummy! Mummy!" called Jill, in a tiny voice. "Do take off your shoes and rescue me! I shall be drowned!"

But of course her mother couldn't hear anything, with the waves making such a noise.

"Well, little girl, I expect the next few waves will smash the castle to pieces," said the crab, poking a leg out of the sand in which he had been burying himself. "I'll say goodbye, I think."

"Oh, don't go!" cried Jill. "I'm frightened!"

But he was gone, and Jill saw him no more on the castle. She looked out to sea. Oh, what big waves there were! The poor castle shivered and shook beneath them, and each time one broke the castle slid

further down into the sea. Soon there was only a small tip of sand left.

Jill looked up the beach at her mother in despair. She saw that Mother had suddenly missed her. She was looking everywhere for her, and calling her.

"Jill! Jill! Come here!" she cried. But Jill couldn't come. And at that very moment the biggest wave of all came along and swept right over the top of the castle. It took Jill along with it, and she gasped and spluttered in fright.

Then she heard Mother's voice again:

"Jill! Jill! Wake up, do! The waves are all over your feet, you silly child!"

Jill opened her eyes – and dear me, what a very peculiar thing! She was lying

on the beach by her sandcastle, and the tide was coming in. A great big wave had broken near it and had run round her feet!

"Why, I must have been asleep and dreamed it all!" said Jill, in astonishment. "Fancy that! But goodness me, what a good thing it was only a dream! I was really getting quite afraid. All right, Mummy, I'm coming. I was dreaming."

Just at that moment a tiny crab looked up out of the wet sand beside her. It was such a knowing little creature that Jill felt sure it was the one that had been on the castle with her.

"Perhaps it wasn't a dream after all," she said. "But it must have been, because there is my castle, still standing!"

"Wouldn't you like to stand on the castle you've made, till the sea is all round it?" asked Mother.

"No, thank you," said Jill, and her mother couldn't think why she didn't want to. But I can guess why, can't you?